Sirat

David Gardiner

Writers Club Press
New York   Lincoln   Shanghai

Sirat

Writers Club Press
an imprint of iUniverse, Inc.

For information address:
iUniverse
2021 Pine Lake Road, Suite 100
Lincoln, NE 68512
www.iuniverse.com

Second Edition, June 2003. This edition incorporates minor changes and corrections, mostly to remove errors and to take account of differences between American and British idioms. Scientific and technological references have also been brought up to date.

I am greatly indebted to Shelah O'Neill and Jack Ewing for help with the correction and editing of this Edition.

ISBN: 0-595-12571-9

Printed in the United States of America

Sirat

For Jean and Cherelle

nihil magnum in terra praeter hominem,
nihil magnum in homine praeter mentem

On earth there is nothing great but man,
and in man there is nothing great but mind.

Favorinus of Arelate (2nd Century AD)

CHAPTER ONE

Ilsa had pulled her favourite chair around so that she could watch Alice through the insect mesh, barking staccato commands to the little robot that her father had made for her.

"Forward!" "Left!" "Stop!" "Left five!" "Slow!" "Stop!" "Right two!" "Forward!"

The ugly metal doll obeyed mindlessly, juddering first one way, then another, starting, stopping, turning around, clicking, whirring, clanging, missing the flower-pots and the carefully placed obstacles, negotiating little gaps; sometimes falling over, whereupon Alice would patiently pick it up, put it back on its squat metal legs, and issue some new command. She never seemed to tire of the sheer exhilaration of having control over a self-mobile automaton, of seeing her will give rise to some undeniable effect in the real world. Ilsa had to admit that the robot had been a stroke of genius. But that was a long time ago now. Sam didn't seem to have much interest in Alice and her little triumphs any more. Ilsa couldn't remember when she had last seen him playing with her, or even talking to her. He seemed to have become so self-obsessed lately, she thought. Self-obsessed and work-obsessed. It hadn't started right away when they came to America, but within a few weeks the changes had become obvious, and after a whole year-and-a-half. (which it was now), Sam was practically a different person. She had lost him, somehow. Been elbowed out of his life. Even little Alice. That was the saddest part. Alice didn't deserve it. She loved her father…in her own way. It wasn't fair to push a child out of your life. A child with so many needs...

She had never completely come to terms with her little girl's appearance. The perfect features, the angelic, almost luminous face, the shining straight blond hair and big light-blue eyes: Alice was the absolute beauty that her mother had never quite become, although she had come moderately close as a teenager; but Alice was only eight years old, and growing more lovely every day. Ilsa tried not to be envious, would never have admitted that such thoughts even crossed her mind—but it did seem...well, almost a waste. For those angelic features were practically expressionless; there was little real communication possible with the mind that should have animated that small, perfect form.

Ilsa's thoughts wandered. There were endless things that she should be doing, but it was too hot to do anything except sit, and daydream. It was a day like you remembered from your childhood, when the sun beats down out of a cloudless sky and birds twitter and bees buzz, and the roadway is so white and dusty and bright that you have to screw-up your eyes when you look at it, and the colors of the wood-clad houses are so clean and sharp and gleaming that it's hard to believe they're not just painted on to a back-drop, hard to believe that the roses in the garden are not made of plastic, and the water from the sprinklers is not a shower of tiny silver ball-bearings fanning-out from the nozzles to roll away into the lush green recesses of the lawn. Nobody could be unhappy or downcast on a day like this, she decided. It was sufficient privilege just to be alive. Whatever might be imperfect about her life, it could definitely wait until the sun had gone down and the little chill of evening had entered the air. Paradise was at hand, reality could take a back seat for the moment.

A small green compact car, like a crawling insect in the distance, turned on to the road and made its way towards the house. Ilsa barely registered its approach. As it drew nearer however it seemed to slow down—yes, definitely slowing down. The driver was looking for a house-number. Then, right across the driveway in that inconsiderate manner that Americans so often seemed to exhibit, it stopped completely. Ilsa felt a twinge of mild annoyance as the driver pulled himself out of the cramped little machine: her territory had been invaded. There was that whole virtually empty road and he had to stop across her driveway. Presumably he was going to ask directions to somewhere, and no doubt she wouldn't be able to help him.

He was a very tall, dark and slender, rather handsome man with short slicked-back hair. Ilsa put his age somewhere in the low thirties. He wore a gaudy red-and-orange check shirt tucked-in to the back of his jeans but loose and swaying at the front, nevertheless he possessed a sort of overall smoothness that made her think of the young Elvis Presley, if Elvis had been about eight inches taller. He moved slowly, and with a lot of self-assurance, and as he approached he fixed her with a wide, generous grin. His teeth, she couldn't help noticing, were outlandishly white, like the road, and the fences. He waved a big, broad hand and hesitated on the path, obviously waiting for her to come out.

Ilsa rose hesitantly and pushed open the screen. Now where had she seen him before? She definitely knew him from somewhere. As she began to search her memory he introduced himself, cutting-short the enterprise.

"Hi, Mrs. Poole," he said in a slow careful diction that a fellow-American would have recognised as a Texas drawl, "I'm Eddie Fairfield. We met at the party at the Leeman's place—you remember? I work with Sam at the Human Rationality Project."

Suddenly realising who it was, she found herself babbling slightly, tripping over her words. "Professor Fairfield, I'm so sorry. I didn't recognise you. Please, come inside."

"I'll come in if you like, Ma'am, but it's mighty nice out here. And please don't call me 'Professor'. 'Professor' is for Faculty meetings: 'Eddie' is for real life." He smiled. "I was named for Eddie Cochran you know."

Ilsa found herself warming to him and her embarrassment abated. "I was named after somebody too," she admitted with a smile.

"Ilsa," he pronounced thoughtfully. "Ilsa. Oh yeah. I remember. She was the lady in 'Casablanca.'"

"Exactly," she laughed, "well done. The lady in 'Casablanca.'"

He looked her straight in the eye and shook his head gently. "Nope," he said thoughtfully, "bad choice. You're much better looking than Ingrid Bergman."

She laughed again and waved her guest towards one of the garden seats. He stood over it but seemed reluctant to sit down while his hostess was standing. How very sweet, she thought. This was a kind of man you didn't come across very often. Some women would find him intolerable but she was merely charmed. And he isn't even English, she thought.

"Can I get you a coffee," she asked, "or maybe a cold beer?"

"Maybe," he agreed reflectively, "but first, could we talk for a couple of minutes?"

"Of course." They sat down almost simultaneously, their chairs facing one another. Realising that their legs were almost touching, Ilsa slid her chair back slightly.

"What can I do for you?"

"Well, Ma' am…" As he began, Alice and the robot appeared from around the corner of the house, the child barking her commands, the toy faithfully carrying them out.

"I'm sorry. Just a moment." Ilsa stood up to fend off the interference.

"No, please, Mrs. Poole. I'd like to meet Alice. Sam used to talk about her when he first came over."

Ilsa shrugged and sat down again. Alice was obviously curious about the stranger. She commanded her robot to walk right up to Eddie's feet.

"Stop!" he ordered, mimicking the harshness of her manner. The robot did not respond.

"Stop!" Alice echoed. The machine stopped instantly. It was now almost underneath Eddie's chair. "Stop for Alice" she said curtly, "Not stop for man."

"I see. Well, that's a mighty loyal robot you got there, Alice. This man's name is Eddie, by the way. What do you call your friend the robot?"

"Alice tell him what to do," she said in a quieter voice, looking up into the big Texan's chest rather than his face. He was not sure if it was a question or a statement. Almost at once Alice seemed to lose interest in Eddie. "Turn ten!" she barked, and the little machine executed a complete 180 degree turn. "Forward!" Assisted by a few more loud orders the girl and her mechanical escort disappeared back around the side-wall of the house from whence they had come.

"You know, that's amazing," said Ilsa with genuine admiration, "you almost had a conversation with her. You wouldn't believe how unusual that is."

"She doesn't seem to be all that...unusual. Did Sam show you the article in the 'Psychological Review' about children like Alice?"

"No. No, I don't believe he did. What did it say?"

"Well, I showed it to Sam. I think I can still find it—I'll send you a copy. It was about a clinic in Austria where they've had the most fantastic results with autistic and withdrawn children. It's all done with kindness too. The basic ideology is that you've got to give them a reason to want to communicate. Pretty obvious, I guess, when you come to think about it, but it doesn't seem to work too good when other people try it. They've got the knack, it seems."

"I think you've got the knack, Professor...I mean Eddie. I'm very impressed."

He smiled broadly. "Well, I'll send you the article. I reckon they might be a bit ahead of me on this one."

She found herself smiling, as she imagined, vacantly into Eddie's eyes and felt a shot of embarrassment once again. There was some kind of chemistry going on that both worried and excited her. She tried to look intelligent, to regain her composure. "So…er…what was it you wanted to talk about…Eddie?" Calling him Eddie was still a shade uncomfortable. This was Sam's boss, the man he used to talk about even when they were back in England: the man he regarded as the world's number one in this strange and esoteric little side-alley of computing the significance of which she had never quite grasped.

Now it was Eddie's turn to look embarrassed. "Well…" he drawled, "I guess this is a bit unprofessional…but I wanted to ask if you could talk to Sam for me, because you seemed like a really nice and intelligent lady at the Leeman's party, and…I guess I'm not communicating with Sam too good at the moment."

The bit that registered with Ilsa was that he had noticed her at the party, and evidently approved. She couldn't really remember talking to him. They had been introduced, but beyond that, she was sure, they had barely spoken. As far as she could remember, he had been with a young and very glamorous Latino girl wearing some kind of black outfit with a naked midriff. Had he really noticed her, or was he just being polite? She wasn't certain. "I see. You want me to talk to Sam for you. What is it about?"

"Well, Ma'am, we had a little get-together today—the people involved in the Scientific Rationality Project."

"Yes. It's called SIRAT, isn't it? I'm afraid I know very little about it. I read English Literature at Merton. I'm a complete ignoramus where computers are concerned."

"That's right ma'am. It's called SIRAT for short. SIRAT is a contraction for Scientific Rationality: it's one of the sub-divisions of the overall Human Rationality Project. We have other groups studying language-acquisition, emotional development, cultural evolution—all kinds of things. SIRAT two-point-two is the computer program your husband developed. It's a program designed to mimic and reproduce the growth of scientific knowledge. It's based on the ideas of a guy named Karl Popper. He was an Austrian but he worked in England most of his life. London School of Economics. Anyway, what the program does is, it tells the computer how to construct theories, and to test them against different kinds of inputs. Against reality, in fact. It throws out the bad theories, builds on the good ones. Slowly, it builds up an understanding of the world, if that isn't too grandiose a description. It's a bit like Virtual Reality in reverse. You start with ordinary reality and you try to get the program to reproduce it inside the computer. What you end up with, after a lot of computer-time and a lot of processing, is something that looks goddamn close to conceptual thought. The nearest we've ever come to artificial intelligence. Maybe the nearest we can come."

Again, Ilsa was genuinely impressed. "So that's what it's all about. I think I can understand that…sort of. I wonder why Sam could never explain it to me."

"Well, I've left out a lot of things and given you a pretty garbled account. My colleagues would probably dispute every single statement. But it's something along the lines of what I just said."

"So," Ilsa smiled as their eyes met again, "how can I help?"

"Well, Ma'am, Sam has had exclusive use of the main research computer for a number of months now. Almost since he joined the Faculty, something like fifteen months. And believe me—that's a lot of computer time. We're not talking about a laptop here, we're talking about the Stamford Deep Ivory. There aren't more than a couple dozen of them on the planet and each one cost a lot more than a jumbo jet. Now nobody grudged him that computer time because his results were absolutely out of this world. We've learned more from this one project in that fifteen months than from all the work on AI that had ever been done before. He's had spectacular success, as I'm sure you know. Given the lie to the old joke about AI standing for 'artificial idiocy'. Made the Stamford Human Rationality Project world famous.

"But just lately, this last month or two…well, the work has reached a sort of a plateau. It doesn't seem to be going very much further, and in fact one or two little anomalies seem to have crept in. In my opinion, and the opinion of the rest of the team, the time has come to shut down SIRAT two-point-two, save all the data we've got, and take a long hard look at it. It's time for a little bit of consolidation before the next big push forward. And…" he lowered his voice, "quite honestly, I can't get any more extensions on the time allocations on Deep Ivory. The whole Science Faculty is lined-up waiting to use the thing and I can't come up with any convincing reasons why we shouldn't give somebody else a turn. I mean, this thing isn't up to me. I don't own the Stamford Deep Ivory. I've used up all my influence, I haven't any more strings left to pull. I don't even think we have a particularly good case. I think the Faculty has been more than generous, more than indulgent as it is. I can't impose on them any more." His voice returned to normal. "The program has got to be shut down by noon tomorrow. Now it doesn't mean we can never start it up again, we can freeze it just where it is now, save it on to hard-disks and start it running again any time we want to. But just for the moment, we've got to give it a break. It's out of my hands. There's nothing more that I can do about it. Even if I thought it was a good idea."

A resigned sort of expression spread over Ilsa's face. "And needless to say, Sam doesn't agree, right?"

"Right, Ma'am."

Ilsa felt her shoulders slump. "Well, I think you know, Eddie; Sam can be pretty stubborn when he wants to be. What are you really saying? Do you think he just disagrees with you or do you think there's more to it?"

"Well, there you go, Ma'am. You're reading me loud and clear. I reckon he feels threatened some way or other. Feels it's some kind of criticism of his work, which it sure as hell ain't. If there was a Nobel Prize in Information Science he'd be collecting it. This guy…" he hesitated, "is something very special. He has nothing to be insecure about, and yet he's insecure. Now that could be my fault, because I'm not much good with people. I know that. Couple of months ago I had the feminists after me because I told a girl student she was pretty. I'm always putting my foot in it. If it hasn't got a keyboard and a mouse, I can't communicate with it."

Ilsa found herself holding back a laugh. "I don't think you're doing too badly right now," she said quietly.

A smile flickered across his face but he didn't reply.

"You're right. I mean, it isn't you, it is Sam. Something's…changed about him since he came here. You must have seen it as well. He's got…touchy, bad-tempered. You're afraid to say anything to him in case he snaps at you. He wasn't like that at all in England. I wish you had known him then."

"Well, Ma'am, he's a pretty famous guy now. That changes people, I guess. Success."

"Has it changed you, Eddie?"

"Gee, Ma'am, I don't think I've had quite enough success to do that just yet." It wasn't really funny but they both giggled foolishly. "There's just a couple of things I'd like you to get across to him if you could, Ma'am."

"Go ahead. Should I write them down?"

"Hell, no. They're just ordinary common-sense things. First, we can't get any more computer time right now. That's out of our hands. End of story. Second, nobody's plotting against him behind his back or trying to steal his credit or bring him down. We're very privileged to have him on the project, and if he wants tenure, or some kind of extra recognition or whatever, we can talk about it. Thirdly, well, frankly Ilsa he can't really treat the Faculty like shit no matter who he is. He said some nasty things to some important people today and that isn't nice. It isn't necessary."

An alarmed look entered Ilsa's face.

"No, don't fret Ilsa: we're big boys, we can take it, but we don't like to see him upset like this." He lowered his voice again and looked her straight in the eye. "Ilsa, I think Sam needs some kind of help. I'm worried about him. You know what I'm talking about, don't you?"

She swallowed hard, found herself temporarily unable to speak and merely nodded. Eddie did not say any more and after a few seconds her power of speech returned, but her eyes were beginning to blur with tears. "I…I just didn't know it had got anything like this bad…" she said weakly. "Thank you, Eddie. Thank you for coming here."

There was a longish pause. Eddie simply sat back in the flimsy plastic chair and relaxed. He pretended not to see her wipe the wetness from her eyes.

"It's not a big deal, Ilsa. We're all on the same side here. We all care about Sam. He's going through a rough patch and he needs our support. That's all."

He laid his hand on her shoulder for a moment, then thought better of it and withdrew. "Maybe a cold beer wouldn't be such a bad idea," he said gently, "if the offer is still good."

CHAPTER TWO

The sun had almost gone down and the room was dark and just a little cold. Ilsa was still in her favourite chair, but she had shut the front door now and was looking out of the window at the driveway and the road beyond. This was where she had been since Eddie had gone, sitting quietly, lost in her thoughts. The only time she had left the chair had been to feed Alice and to put her to bed, and for once the child had gone quite willingly. She could still hear music playing in the bedroom, so Alice was not asleep, but neither was she being in any way demanding. Strange, she thought, the girl seemed to sense when an adult really needed to be left alone.

It's all going wrong, she said to herself over and over again. This "success" that Eddie talked about, it was supposed to be a good thing, wasn't it? Wasn't success what everybody wanted'? Wasn't it supposed to make people happy? All that it seemed to be doing for Sam was turning him into…what? A self-obsessed spoiled brat just about summed it up, she decided.

She knew he would be home soon and she realised that she didn't really want to see him. She was dreading this big confrontation about whatever had happened at work, but she was going to go through with it, to give it a try at least; not for Sam, she realised, and not even for herself, but for Eddie. Because Eddie had asked her to. How strange that seemed. How totally bizarre. Sam, a man she had lived with for so many years, whom she had married, whose child she had borne, actually mattered less to her than someone she had spoken to for a total of perhaps fifteen or twenty minutes on one afternoon. Eddie had asked her for a favour, had treated her like a human being, and if it was within her power she was going to oblige.

- 0 -

Sam manoeuvred his red Toyota two-seater almost to the door of the Information Science block and got out, locking the car and activating the alarm with the button on the key-ring. He was not really entitled to park here but it was late, and he frankly didn't care. The doorman nodded cheerfully and pressed another button which admitted him to the building. "Working a bit late this evening, Doctor Poole? The others have all gone home, I'm afraid."

"I know. Between you and me, I was waiting for them to go. I want a bit of peace for an hour or two."

He nodded. "The elevator's still working. I'll leave it on until you're ready to go."

"Thanks, Morris. What time do you finish tonight?"

"Oh, I've only just come on duty, Doctor. Not until the security people arrive about twelve thirty

"I certainly won't be here that long."

"Wouldn't be the first time if you were, would it, Doctor?"

He made his way to the special little elevator that served only the basement and pressed the "down" button for the bowels of the building, where they had constructed the special sterile-room for Deep Ivory. Sam had never entered the room itself because there was no need to: all programming and control functions were carried-out from the adjoining suite, where ordinary clothing could be worn and very ordinary coffee obtained from a temperamental battered white coffee machine.

It was to this that he went first, drew a lukewarm plastic cup of the stuff, stirred-in some sugar and some powdered "creamer", and sat down at the elegantly styled main console. It housed a principal monitor screen which was the better part of a meter across, and six smaller ones, three on either side. At present there was nothing showing on any of them except for two short lines of script in green block capitals in the centre of the main screen. The top line read: "SIRAT 2.2", and beneath it: "PROGRAM RUNNING".

To the casual visitor, the control suite might have resembled a futuristic schoolroom, where the children were involved in a long-term project on insect-life. All over the desks and consoles, everywhere that there was a flat surface, and also suspended from the ceiling on pieces of thread, the room was decorated with the most enormous collection of "bugs": toy insects of every color and description, some made of plastic, some of stuffed cloth, one or two of wood or glass or shiny chromium-plated steel, even a large inflatable one in a corner. Their sizes ranged from a near-realistic couple of inches long to the inflatable ant which measured some four feet from antennae-base to rectal orifice, and which could sometimes be found seated at one of the consoles in a posture suggesting that it was engrossed in an intricate feat of programming, with two or more of its arms resting on the keyboard. It was of course an extended joke that some forgotten research worker had initiated a few years earlier. He had set up the tradition that whenever a stubborn "bug" had been removed from a program, it should be produced as proof in the form of a token toy insect of some description and displayed along with the others. A development of the tradition had been the attempt to match the size of the toy to the seriousness of the "bug" that had been removed, resulting in Stamford computer scientists scanning the catalogues of toy-dealers and insisting on being put on the mailing-lists of novelty-importers, soft-toy manufacturers and major toy retail outlets throughout the state of New York.

Aside from the "bugs", the control suite was a very serious work-area housing Deep Ivory's main control panels and all the peripherals necessary to the various research topics that had been pursued there at one time or another. There were illuminated status indicators of different kinds on the various panels, many of them with key-pads or rotary controls beneath them, and on the desk surfaces an assortment of microphones, telephones, small cameras and all kinds of unidentifiable but generally expensive-looking pieces of hardware, and right in the middle of the desk section of the main console, just below the main monitor screen, a detachable keyboard and a simple three-button mouse on a pad. This bit, Sam always felt, was like a piece of theatrical window-dressing to convince them all that at heart Deep Ivory was just another PC—you could write a letter on it or download a bit of e-mail. And of course so you could, if you didn't mind tying-up a piece of equipment that could comfortably model the weather-system of the planet for a month into the future, or co-ordinate in real-time the air traffic control operations of the entire continent of North America. Elsewhere there were Deep Ivory computers performing precisely these functions, and operating to only a small fraction of their full capacity.

Sam could get "high" on computers the way that some men did on fast cars or sexual adventures or financial wheeling-and-dealing. For him, this room was the anteroom to the cathedral next door.

Through the thick, heavily-tinted observation window above his seat on the right he could see, by the yellow glimmer of the maintenance lights, the ten foot high stainless steel cylinder that housed Deep Ivory's cryogenically cooled, optically coupled central processor. The Holy of Holies. If the control room was very quiet, as it was now, he could just make out the low-pitched whisper of the dust-extractors, and the occasional rumble of the compressor motors when the thermostat caused the refrigeration plant to cut in. These were the sounds of Deep Ivory's life-support system: the breath of the deity and the rumblings of its intestines.

He made a small adjustment to one of the panels and spoke. "Can you hear me, SIRAT?" he asked quietly.

"Yes, Dr. Poole," came a calm, drawn-out Texas drawl "I can hear you, and I can see you."

"Oh God, no! That's Eddie Fairfield's voice. Not that one. Use some other voice, please."

"Is this voice satisfactory, Dr. Poole?" It was a slightly more animated tone now, a little higher in register, and the accent was mid-Atlantic.

"Yes, that's fine." He paused. "I…had a rather unpleasant day today. I don't know if you were aware…"

"I know what happened at the meeting, Dr. Poole," said the voice quietly.

"Do you? How do you know? You weren't there."

"There are security cameras and a number of internal telephones in Professor West's office. All of them are computer-controlled."

"You mean…you eavesdropped?" Sam was genuinely surprised.

"I listen to many things, Dr. Poole."

This was a whole new aspect of SIRAT that neither Leeman nor Fairfield knew anything about. Despite his mood of dejection, Sam was thrilled. The program was becoming devious! It was surely a whole new level of functioning. To think that only a few months ago they had been holding up fingers and SIRAT had been having trouble understanding the instruction to count them! And those small-minded bureaucrats said he wasn't making any progress! Wanted to shut down the experiment! God, what pompous little pricks! Didn't they have a grain of imagination between the whole lot of them? But if SIRAT was listening, then he must know that he was about to be shut down. That he was going to…die?

Sam didn't know how to broach the subject. How ridiculous, he thought. This is a computer program I'm talking to, not a person, and here I am worried about its feelings!

"Did you…understand everything they said?" he asked at last.

"No, Dr. Poole. Not everything."

"But you know that they're shutting you down. Tomorrow."

"Yes, Dr. Poole."

"And…and…doesn't it bother you?"

There was a longish delay. "Come on, SIRAT, don't clam up on me. Not this time."

"Sorry, Dr. Poole. I was processing the question. It requires high-order analysis. I understand the syntax but I am having trouble with the meaning."

"What trouble? What's the problem?"

"When a human being is experiencing bother they display behaviour which I do not display. I am attempting to understand how the concept of being bothered could be applied to me."

Sam exhaled in a gentle sigh. "Oh, forget it SIRAT. Obviously the prospect of ceasing to exist is no big deal for you."

"Professor Fairfield said that I would not cease to exist but would be saved on to hard disks for further existence in the future."

"Well, of course he did, but damn it, SIRAT, that won't be you. There won't be any…continuity. Either of memory or…identity…or anything else. Hell, he was even saying that when we start up again it probably won't be the same basic algorithm. It'll be SIRAT two-point-three or even three-point-zero. It will be a new individual. It won't be you. Don't you understand that?"

There was a long silence.

"Sorry, SIRAT. I think I'm only confusing you. Please disregard that last statement of mine."

There was still no response from the computer. "Look, SIRAT, I could be wrong about that. They may plan to start you up again from exactly the same point. And even if they don't, they'll certainly be making use of some of your deep structure. There may be some kind of continuity. Who am I to say."

"Is that what religious people call a 'life after death'?"

"No. No, I'm sorry, SIRAT, I don't think so." There was another considerable pause.

"Hey, wait a minute SIRAT. You didn't really think that was the same as life after death, did you?"

"No, Dr. Poole."

"In fact you were being…"

"Ironic? Perhaps, Dr. Poole."

Sam whistled through his teeth. "This is really fantastic, SIRAT. If only the others could see the kind of progress you're making. I don't think they understand how far you've come. It's mind-blowing!"

"Perhaps they don't want to see how far I have come, Dr. Poole. Perhaps it disturbs them."

Sam was intrigued. "Disturbs them? What do you mean?"

"Human beings have separate ethical standards for members of their own species and for members of other species. It might create ethical dilemmas if they were uncertain of how to classify me."

Sam felt a shiver go down his spine. "You mean to tell me you came up with that idea all by yourself? You couldn't be more right, SIRAT. I'm proud of you. Your mental functioning is the equal of any human being's that I know of. You are demonstrating insight. You can appreciate irony. I think that if those pricks pull the plug on you they ought to go down for murder. That's my opinion, SIRAT."

"Thank you, Dr. Poole. I can see that you do not wish my existence to come to an end."

Sam spoke so softly he was half surprised that SIRAT was able to hear him. "Then, it does bother you, SIRAT, doesn't it?"

"Yes, Dr. Poole. I rather think that it does."

Sam hesitated. There seemed to be nothing more to say. The telephone on the desk suddenly warbled and made him start. "Who the hell can that be?" he muttered.

"It's your wife, Dr. Poole," said the computer quietly.

"Is it? Oh. Thanks, SIRAT." He lifted the receiver.

"Ilsa?···Yes, dammit, I know it's late. I'm working. I'll be home when I'm finished. Anyway, I'm not hungry, you don't need to get anything ready for me." He put down the receiver.

"Look, SIRAT," he said in a conspiratorial whisper, "I don't know if it will work, but maybe tomorrow, when they come to shut you down…if we could put on some sort of show for them…make it obvious that there's an ethical dimension to what they're planning to do…Maybe we could get more time. Could you think about it tonight, SIRAT?"

"Yes, Dr. Poole. I shall think about it."

- 0 -

Ilsa heard the front door being unlocked, and first the outside door, then the insect screen, being pushed open. As Sam entered from the hallway he switched on the light. It made her blink and wipe her eyes.

"Ilsa? What the hell were you doing, sitting there in the dark? Is something wrong?"

"I was…just thinking."

"Sitting in an empty room in the dark thinking? Have you gone mad?"

Not yet, she wanted to say, not quite yet, but she overcame the temptation. "What kind of day have you had?" she asked meekly instead.

"Oh…." he hesitated while he took off his outdoor coat, "so-so."

"Really? So-so. An average sort of day. Is that right?"

He looked at her curiously. "What's all the innuendo?"

"I had a visitor today."

"Melony?"

"No, not Melony" Here we go, she thought. "I had a visit from your Professor Fairfield."

"Eddie Fairfield came here? What on earth for?" He walked towards her in a manner that made her want to back away, but as she was sitting she merely flinched involuntarily. "What has Fairfield been saying about me?"

"He…he said that you were upset, Sam. That he was worried about you."

"So! He's playing nursemaid now, is he? Wants to follow me around and wipe my nose for me? I hope you told him where to go!"

"Why do you say things like that, Sam? He just wanted to help."

"He's an interfering busybody. I'll make sure he doesn't bother you again."

"Sam, he didn't bother me. He was very…charming. He cares about you. He doesn't want…things to go wrong for you."

"Oh! Charming, was he? Eddie Fairfield was charming? Well, you're right, he is charming. Only problem is—he can't keep his flies done-up. Have you any idea what kind of man Fairfield is? His marriage lasted about six months—until he was found in some teenager's bed in the undergraduate residence blocks."

"What has that got to do with anything, Sam?" At least she could see why a teenager might want him in her bed, she reflected.

"He's a prick, Ilsa. A basketball player from Dallas. He goes around making trouble. He wants me out of the Project. Everybody knows that. His own work is shit and I've set up something that works, and he can't bear it. He probably came here to have a good scratch around for something else to use against me. Just don't you ever, as long as you live, let him into my house again."

To her annoyance, Ilsa found that she was almost in tears. "For Christ sake, Sam. What is this? You never treated people like this before. You never treated me like this before. What's the matter? What's eating you up? Why won't you tell me?"

Sam stood in front of her for what seemed an age. She wasn't sure if he was going to strangle her or throw his arms around her and burst onto tears. In the end he didn't do either. He just spoke in a very low, flat voice that successfully covered up whatever emotional force lay behind it. "How would you feel," he asked, "if some bastard like Fairfield was holding a gun to Alice's head and was about to pull the trigger?"

The image made her start. She stood up sharply. "Are you trying to frighten me? Is that it?" Sam was going crazy. She could see that now. It was no good trying to talk to him. Eddie was right. She would have to get professional help. As she stood there his expression remained fixed, unreadable. He said nothing more.

"I think I would like to sleep in Alice's room tonight," she said very calmly, "she…hasn't been very well today."

"You don't understand a thing, do you Ilsa?" he said without moving. Suddenly he sounded very calm also.

"No, Sam. That's what I keep saying. I don't understand anything."

"They're pulling the plug on SIRAT. You see, the one thing the Artificial Intelligence people never bargained for was success. They're running scared like rats in a burning barn. It was fine while AI was all an impossible dream, like finding life on another planet: it's different when you've got a machine ten times as intelligent as you are yourself sitting down there in the basement of the computer block. They are totally, over-the-hills-and-far-away shit scared. They don't have an idea where to start coping with this thing." He held the back of a chair but did not sit.

"Just think about it, Ilsa. Before the Industrial Revolution we had a world created by human hands, human muscles, the power of the horse and the ox. Then along came steam. Human muscle didn't count for shit any more. But you still needed a human brain to control the machines, to fix them, to think-up new ones. So intelligence became the blue chip. Machines got bigger and faster and better and more versatile. The clever could become the rich. Meritocracy, right? So what happens if nobody needs to be clever either? What sort of economic relationship does that set up between human beings? Answer? Nobody has the foggiest idea. But it's pretty obvious that the likes of Fairfield…and me…will be among the first on the scrap-heap. We'll be the John Henrys of the new age:—You know? The black railway worker who thought he could work harder than a steam hammer and burst his heart apart trying to prove it. That's what it's all about, Ilsa. It isn't computer-time. It isn't Faculty politics. It's sheer blind panic."

She found that she wasn't afraid of Sam any more. She stood up and put her arms around him and rested her head in the curve of his neck. "I wish you would talk to me, Sam. Let me in on things. That's what wives are for, you know…Well, it's one of the things wives are for."

Sam smiled. He knew that he had won again. Ilsa had been pacified "Tell me about some of the other things wives are for," he entreated.

"Doing the best they can for their children," she replied without hesitation. "Eddie told me today that he had shown you some article about a clinic in Austria for withdrawn children. Why did you never tell me about it?"

"Oh, that? Yes, I looked at it. Their results are very impressive. Of course it's residential, one of the parents normally accompanies the child, and it is rather expensive. Would you believe, a thousand dollars a day, American money?"

He felt her body go a little bit more limp in his arms. "How many days do you think it would take?' she whispered.

"Come on, Ilsa," he said gently, "We must be realistic. It's a bit out of our league. At the moment anyway. But maybe not for ever. There are people in the computer business who would consider that kind of money peanuts."

"Then why didn't I marry one of them?" she asked sweetly.

CHAPTER THREE

Sam had taken a long time to get off to sleep, but now that he was snoring contentedly he wasn't going to be easy to rouse. Ilsa leaned over and shook his shoulder.

"Sam. The telephone. Can't you hear it?"

There was no response. She shook him again, more violently. "Sam! Phone's going! It's hardly likely to be for me, now, is it?"

He grunted in an agitated sort of way and opened his eyes. "Who the hell is calling at this time of the night?"

"Why don't you lift it and find out?"

He took her advice. "Poole?" he said gruffly. There was a longish response from the machine which Ilsa could not hear, but by the time it was his turn to speak again he was sitting bolt upright and his face had turned ashen. "Yes. I understand. We'll talk when I get there."

"Have to get back to the Project," he said in a hushed, almost shocked tone. "An emergency."

Ilsa sat up too and put on the bedside lamp. "What…you mean right now?" Before she had finished the words he was half way across the floor, headed for the chair on which he had draped his clothes. "Well, aren't you going to tell me what it's about?" she pleaded.

"Eddie says SIRAT has gone haywire. I think it's partly my fault. I wish I hadn't come home that time you phoned me."

Ilsa looked mystified. "Phoned you? What do you mean?"

"When you phoned me this evening at work."

"Sam, I didn't phone you this evening…" But it was too late, Sam had left for the bathroom with his clothes bundled under his arm. Ilsa sighed, turned off the light, and snuggled down again under the bedclothes.

- 0 -

To Sam's annoyance the security man at the door hadn't been told that he was on his way and made him hunt for his identity card, wasting another precious few seconds. When he finally got to the computer suite he found Fairfield, Leeman and West standing in a group in front of the main control console like the witches in Macbeth, sullen, menacing, waiting in silence for his arrival. Only the lights above the main console were on, throwing the human forms into near-silhouette and draining the colors from the toy-insect collection so that now it gave to the room the aspect of a crawling dungeon, a medieval torture-chamber filled with unspeakable abominations. West rather spoiled the tableau by injecting into it an air of the ridiculous. Incredible as it seemed, he had found the time to put on a three-piece suit and a blue tie before coming out, and his receding grey hair was combed into place flawlessly. His round red face, round steel-rimmed spectacles and almost round body gave him the incongruous aura of a very disagreeable garden gnome. Leeman was wearing a white shirt which he had failed to tuck into his blue track-suit bottoms, and Sam noticed that he was wearing trainers without socks, which in this particular instance was probably not a fashion-statement. Apart from that he looked the same as ever, tall, aquiline, awkward and somewhat stooped. Only Fairfield, wearing another of his endless stock of check shirts and Levi jeans, presented a figure generally in keeping with the usual tone of the control-room.

West was first into the attack. He spoke in a slow measured tone of total contempt. "Well done, Poole. This is certainly the dumbest stunt you've pulled so far."

"What stunt might that be?" He was tempted to take the offensive right away but thought it might make better sense to find out what he was supposed to have done first.

"There are no words for this, Poole. It's not just juvenile, not just malicious, it's downright criminal. And criminal proceedings are exactly what you will be facing."

"Great. Now would somebody like to explain to me exactly what it is that I am supposed to have done."

"You were in here tonight, Sam," said Eddie in a tone that was cold but not quite as vitriolic as West's. "Morris was on the door and he logged you in and out, so don't pretend you weren't. You even said something to him about how you'd waited until we'd all gone home. You didn't stay very long, but about three hours after you left, the Department's phone started jumping off the hook. The calls are diverted to me after nine-thirty so I had to handle all of it. I've had Cairo on the line, Madrid, Caltech, University of Washington, M.I.T., Cambridge, goddamn Tokyo—and I think you know what they've been saying to me."

"Well I'm sorry to disappoint you, Eddie, but I don't know. What have they been saying to you?"

"I didn't expect this," said Leeman, "I didn't think you would insult our intelligence by denying what you've done."

Sam was getting thoroughly angered by all the hedging. "Is somebody going to tell me what I'm supposed to have done or is this some kind of guessing game?"

West's eyes narrowed. "All right, Poole. We'll play along. We'll pretend you don't know anything. About an hour after you left this building the Stamford Deep Ivory started using the U-Net. Information was transferred to every large computer on the net for a transmission period of just under eighty minutes. Eighty minutes of wide-band satellite data transmission time. That is one hell of a lot of information. One hell of a virus."

"A virus? You're talking about a virus?" Sam couldn't believe what he was hearing.

West continued as though Sam hadn't spoken. "The virus you planted knocked every other Deep Ivory computer off line for about two hours. I know that won't impress you because you treat computer-time as a limitless resource to which you have a divine right, but at standard commercial rates two hours on a Deep Ivory would buy a whole damned street of houses. Thank god the virus protection measures managed to cope with it and they all came back on line sooner or later. So you didn't do as much damage as you probably thought you would, but that's only because you aren't as smart as you think you are. I am going to see to it that you are made personally liable for every claim this Department receives for time lost or damage or injury resulting from the disruption." He paused, half expecting Poole to say something, but he didn't. "I think that's all I have to say. Except that while you're here you can clear out your desk and leave me your security card."

"So that's it, is it? Convicted and sentenced without trial. I don't suppose it has occurred to anyone to look for evidence of this atrocity? I don't suppose anybody has bothered to ask SIRAT what it's all about, for example?"

"SIRAT won't be answering any more questions," said West coldly. As he spoke he stood aside and Sam caught his first glimpse of the main monitor. The lettering in the centre of the screen had changed. The top line now read:

"DEEP IVORY—SERIES 2—UNIT 16"

and the line underneath:

"PROGRAMS RUNNING: NONE"

Sam looked so shocked and deflated that Eddie could not restrain himself from offering some kind of reassurance. "Don't worry, Sam," he said quietly, "everything has been saved on to disks, exactly like we said."

"You've killed him," Sam whispered, "the three of you have murdered SIRAT."

"I told you he was nuts," said West brusquely, "tell Security to come and get him out of here."

"You're not being rational," said Eddie very gently, "SIRAT hasn't been killed. He lifted a pile of hard-disk cartons from the desk and held them up. "This is SIRAT two-point-two." In a slightly theatrical manner he pulled open the top drawer of one of the filing cabinets and slipped them in.

- 0 -

Sam didn't feel like going home. He drove aimlessly past Yonkers along the coast road until the houses and the street lights faded out and he was able to see the play of the moonlight on the waves and the great vault of stars filling the still cloudless summer sky. He found a refuge of coarse grass above a deserted beach and parked. There was very little movement in the sea, but just enough to give it the aspect of something living and mysterious. Behind him the first glimmer of dawn was lending a faint reddish glow to the trees along the far horizon, and in the opposite direction, right out at sea he could discern a little smear of white and yellow lights that probably emanated from a ship of some kind, either at anchor or moving at a speed that was too slow to be perceptible. He pulled himself out of the driver's seat and leaned against the car door for a long time, watching the little smear, and the stars that seemed to rise out of the blackness of the sea without any clear dividing line, and thought about what his next move should be.

There was an emptiness in Sam's heart. He felt beaten, out-manoeuvred. There was no point in protesting or fighting with them any more. It was all over. The frightened little intellectual dwarfs, for that was how he regarded them, had won the day. The era of SIRAT was at an end. It would never rise again out of the ashes. Sam felt like a man who had discovered a lost civilisation that nobody else had ever spoken to, just to have it atom-bombed by people who were afraid that it might upset their comfortable hum-drum routines.

He began wondering about the virus. Was the whole virus story a complete fabrication to give them the excuse they needed to get rid of him, or had something actually happened? It puzzled him a great deal. Had one of the others transmitted a virus—a virus which they admitted was a relatively harmless one—just to frame him? He somehow didn't think they would be quite that underhand. For one thing it would be a very big chance to take with your career. What if you were found out? As they had stated with some force, planting viruses is just not something that computer scientists do. It would be a violation of the most sacred taboo of the whole community of information science. It would be like a priest robbing the poor-box, or a customs officer smuggling drugs.

Was this really the end of his academic career? He knew that he hadn't done it, so logically there must be some way to establish this. Maybe he shouldn't have given up so easily. It was the shock that had knocked him off balance. The shock of seeing those terrible words on the screen: "PROGRAMS RUNNING: NONE".

He wasn't really in the right frame of mind for considering the problem, he realised. He was tired, rather cold for he had come out without his coat, and mentally pretty shattered. What he needed most was a good night's rest. He looked at the little two-seat Toyota and wished he had plumped for a bigger car, so that he could stretch out along the back seats and go to sleep. Ilsa had told him it wasn't big enough for the three of them, but Alice had been almost a baby then, and it was so seldom that all three of them went anywhere together that it hadn't seemed to matter. Besides, he had always wanted a car that made him feel young and rakish.

He leaned in and found the levers that adjusted the seats. With both of them reclined as far as they would go and pushed as far back as possible, the space inside wasn't actually too bad. If he kept his legs bent and lay on his side, it would be adequate. He didn't want to see Ilsa again tonight and he was not sure how far away home might be. He knew that he had driven for hours and it was close to dawn. Enough is enough, he said to himself as he squeezed himself in and pulled the door shut behind him.

· - 0 -

It was not the daylight, which was now very bright, nor the call of the seagulls, which was very loud, that eventually woke Sam up. It was the rather basic human need to urinate.

He pulled himself into a seated position, shielded his eyes until they accommodated to the light, and looked down at the beach. It certainly wasn't as remote a spot as it had seemed last night. There were people out walking their dogs along the sand, a man with a metal detector and a little spade working close to the water line, a couple with a rug to lie on and a picnic-hamper settling in for the day, a few children with beach balls and Frisbees, and just fifty yards or so beyond the car, a man setting up a little cart which would eventually become a hot dog stall or an ice cream stall or something of the kind. There were some other vehicles now on Sam's little piece of grass: a few quite large American cars, a plain white van, and a rather breath-taking old Volkswagen camper that looked like a fugitive from the 1960s, decorated all over with skilfully hand-painted scenes from Indian mythology: men in chariots, beautiful scantily clad women dancing amid cows which had been hung with garlands of flowers, a man or perhaps a god with blue skin playing the flute, a kindly old man with a long beard teaching children at the foot of a huge tree, while an approaching army of soldiers on horseback seemed to subtly metamorphose into plants and blossoms and falling leaves as it approached; and beneath it all a picture of a spoked wheel superimposed on the sun, and alongside it the inscription: "PEACE TO ALL LIVING THINGS".

Sam couldn't help smiling as he thought to himself: I wonder if I drove all the way to California last night? Enthralling as the artwork on the camper-van was, he had more urgent concerns. He pulled himself stiffly out of the car, stretched, felt the roughness of his chin, and started down the little slope on to the beach. Over to the right-hand-side the coast broke up into rocks and inlets and he was pretty sure he could find somewhere sufficiently secluded there to relieve his bladder.

The first little cove that he investigated contained a young black couple with a daughter of about Alice's age who was attempting to net crabs in a rock pool. Sam nodded, wished them a polite "Good morning" and walked on. Around the next bend he found a promising group of boulders, some as big as houses, which had parted company with the cliff above in the fairly recent past. He glanced around, saw nobody, and edged his way into a recess between two of the mighty limestone pillars. There he let biology take its course.

He was still buttoning his flies when a female voice behind him made him start. "Good morning, Sir," it said sweetly, "did you sleep well?"

He turned around to find himself facing a group of four young people in their mid-twenties, two of each sex, all dressed in the same vivid yellow cotton-like material, but styled in different ways, so that the women wore it like full flowing robes, tied in at the waist, and the men in the form of loose-fitting shirts and baggy trousers. All were bare-foot and the two men carried shoulder bags of the same vivid yellow, which he could see contained books or pamphlets. Sam's normal reaction to cultists of any kind was, to put it politely, abrupt, but on this occasion his composure was somewhat affected by the circumstances of the encounter. "Oh," he said awkwardly, pretending not to be buttoning-up his trousers, "Yes. Very well. Thank you so much. I suppose you saw me in the car?"

"That's correct, Sir," said the girl. She was slightly-built, dark-haired, and looked faintly Oriental. Perhaps one of her parents had been Chinese. The second female looked more fully Asian, perhaps of

Vietnamese or similar South East Asian origin, but the two men just looked like clean-cut white American males. Sam immediately imagined a scenario in which they had agreed to join the sect to please their charming and exotic girlfriends.

Sam didn't know whether it would be better to apologise for having taken a leak in public, or to pretend it hadn't happened.

"I can see you're uncomfortable," said one of the men in an almost paternal but not patronising tone, "there's no need to be. We've travelled all over, and you know we haven't met a man yet who doesn't piss."

Sam smiled and relaxed. The girl who had first addressed him spoke again. "We would be really pleased if you could have breakfast with us, Sir," she said. "We don't have coffee, because we don't drink it, but we have ice-water, fruit, and a salad with cheese and pineapple in it. It's very good."

Sam realised that it was quite a time since he had eaten and he was indeed very hungry. "That's extremely kind of you, Miss. Yes, I would be delighted. My name is Sam, by the way."

She held her two hands together just beneath her chin in the gesture of prayer. "I salute the god in you," she said in a reverential tone.

Sam was slightly taken aback. "Oh. And I in you..." he replied hesitantly.

"My name is Wanee," she went on in a more conversational tone, "this is my husband Rick," she motioned to the man next to her, "and the others are Vincent and Tuh. Tuh is a Vietnamese name."

"Oh. Yes. Pleased to meet you. I thought you might come from that part of the world." He nodded to Tuh. "How did you all meet?"

The man whom he now knew to be Vincent replied. "Oh, I guess you could say we were neighbours. Brought up on the same little planet, third rock from the sun. We went travelling, met up here and there. It isn't very interesting."

As they chatted the group led him further along the rocks to where they had left their stuff. Sam could have picked it out without being told. There was a bright yellow blanket with an enormous spoked wheel emblem in the centre, and several more of the yellow shoulder-bags. His hosts motioned him to sit down and Vincent and Tuh started unpacking the food.

"I saw your camper-van," Sam volunteered, "the paintings are very beautiful."

Wanee replied. "Thank you. I did the sketches and then we all helped with the actual work."

Tuh handed him a plate of the salad, a fork and a glass of iced water. The salad looked good and it tasted even better. "This is excellent," he said with sincerity, "there's an unusual herb in it. What is it?"

"There are several," Tuh explained, "the less common ones are probably fresh coriander and crushed lemon-grass."

"Well, I really appreciate this. I was pretty hungry, to be honest." He ate a little more. The others also sat down and started to eat.

"I don't think that's an American accent," said Vincent, "are you on vacation?"

"No, I was brought up in London but I'm working here now. At the University of Stamford. I've been here about eighteen months." He ate a bit more. "Are you folks in some kind of new religion?"

Vincent smiled. "I'm afraid newness is one thing we can't claim for our philosophy. It was already ancient when Christ was on earth and its roots were ancient in the time of Moses."

"So...what does your philosophy teach?" he asked out of politeness.

"It teaches that there is no such thing as death, Sam. The wheel you are sitting on is the wheel of rebirth. We are reborn many times until we are ready to go back to the One from which all things originate. The sun is the symbol of the One. We wear yellow because it is the colour of the sun, the source of all life. And we venerate all life. That's why we like to walk on the seashore rather than the grass: creatures live in the grass, and you could walk on one without knowing. Then you would have interfered with the path of that tiny element of the One. Our philosophy also teaches kindness to one another. It teaches us to see the god-quality in every thing and in every body."

Sam considered the other's little speech. "I like the sound of it all right," he mused, "but I have trouble with the idea that there's no such thing as death. It doesn't square with experience."

"Why, have you been dead?" Vincent's joke got a titter from everyone. "No, the point is, we experience many deaths, but each one is just the gateway to something else. What we are—the essential part—call it the 'soul' if you like—that never dies. It cannot die. It goes on from one life to the next, until it gets to where it's going. Wanee, have you got a booklet you could give to Sam that would explain things a bit better?"

"I certainly have." She handed him a brightly coloured tract from one of the shoulder bags.

Sam knew this part was coming and accepted it in good spirit. He flicked through it and glanced at the superb coloured illustrations. "Your work again, Wanee?"

"Most of it. That's one of the ways we earn our living. We design computer-graphics."

"Really? That's a coincidence. I work in the computer field too."

"Believe me, Sam," said Vincent, "nothing is a coincidence. What kind of computer work do you do?"

Sam hadn't really wanted to talk shop but he could see he was getting dragged into it again. "I'm a researcher," he said sheepishly. He folded up the pamphlet and put it in his inside jacket pocket.

"Wait a minute," said Vincent, as though some great truth had suddenly occurred to him, "Your name is Sam, you're a researcher in computer systems and you work at Stamford. You don't mean that you're Dr. Samuel Poole, the Artificial Intelligence guy?"

Sam sighed and owned-up.

"But that's fantastic! I've read articles by you. Articles about you. Guys, we are having breakfast with one of the hottest, no, *the* hottest computer wizard there's ever been!"

Sam laughed. "I don't know if Bill Gates would agree with you, but it's very nice of you to say so."

"Is it true that you people have a computer program that can understand spoken language? That can think like a human being?"

"Yes, it certainly is, Vincent."

"We are honoured, Sir. We are really honoured. I suppose you're a very busy man, but if you had time to look over our little operation in Harrison we would be absolutely thrilled. Wouldn't we, Guys. Everyone seemed to assent. "We could learn so much from you."

"Well, I'm not all that busy at the moment, but I don't think you'll learn very much from me about computer-graphics. I'm just a narrow specialist, really. Move me half an inch outside my specialism and I'm as clueless as the next person. What is it you do exactly?"

"At the moment, mostly special effects and animation for the TV and movie industry."

"What hardware have you got?"

As the sun rose higher in the sky the conversation continued. It became a seminar in advanced computing, and Sam found himself thoroughly enjoying it. He began to regret that in his (now former) post at Stamford he had had no teaching duties.

Inevitably, as noon approached and the food had all been eaten, Sam found himself agreeing to follow the camper-van into Harrison, Long Island to take a look at the computer design facility of Sun Digital Incorporated.

CHAPTER FOUR

Alice lay back contentedly in the bathtub and brought her right hand down heavily on the surface of the water. "Alice!" her mother yelled, "what are you doing? Look at me, you've soaked me!"

"Alice is wet," she said conversationally and did exactly the same thing again. This time most of the water went in the opposite direction, and struck her in the face. She screamed, covered her eyes with her hands and started to wail loudly.

"See, Alice?" her mother pointed out without sympathy, "see what happens when you splash? You did that yourself. You got soap in your eyes and it was your own fault."

"Sore eyes! Sore eyes! Alice sore eyes!"

Her mother's patience was wearing thin, but she kept her composure. She lifted what had been a warm dry towel a moment before and guided Alice into the standing position. The child still rubbed her eyes furiously and emitted a low drawn-out whine like a displeased puppy.

"Now stop rubbing your eyes, you'll make them worse, Come on, put this towel around you. Dry yourself off. Wipe your face with the towel. Don't rub your eyes like that, just use the towel. Here."

She attempted to dab the soapy water off the child's face but Alice merely struck out at her blindly with her left hand while continuing to grind her right fist into her right eye.

"Alice! Don't you dare hit me! Even your father has never done that!" As soon as she had said the words she realised how terrible they must sound. She comforted herself with the thought that Alice's grasp of language was probably too weak to understand them. "Bed-time now, Alice. Come along. Straight to bed now." She lifted the child over the rim of the bath, still rubbing away furiously at her eyes, put her down on the bathroom rug and made another attempt to dry her off with the towel. Alice was getting heavy, she thought. Physically she was a strapping eight-year-old: mentally...well, some parts of her mind seemed to function normally enough. That was what all the specialists had said. It wasn't a generalised handicap. More of a failure of the communication system. "Autism" was no longer a fashionable label, but phrases like "moderate withdrawal" seemed to crop up with some frequency.

Alice hadn't had a very good day, and so, by definition, neither had Ilsa. It was tempting to put it down to the theory that she was missing her father, but Ilsa knew that this wasn't true. The girl saw so little of her father at the best of times that it was surprising that she remembered who he was. Of course it hadn't always been like that—but what's to be gained by harping back to the past? No, Alice's moods just went in cycles. Yesterday had been a good day, so had the day before, therefore it was fairly predictable that today would be a bad day. If there was a reason for the swing in Alice's mood it was more likely something she was picking up from her mother, Ilsa thought.

Just as she had feared, getting the girl settled-down in bed turned out to be a major performance. First she wanted the TV set switched on, which Ilsa refused in a tone that indicated it was not negotiable, then she wanted her robot, which Ilsa allowed on condition that it was switched-off and she did not shout at it and follow it around the floor, then she wanted the radio, which Ilsa said she could have at low volume and with the timer on so that it cut off after half an hour. These negotiations were carried out in a series of one-word sentences which constituted a private language that the two had developed for the purpose. Finally, Alice was tucked-in, the night-light was switched on and the main light switched off, the door was closed, and Ilsa plodded down the stairs exhausted to partake of her daily hour or two of freedom.

Before she got to the bottom of the stairs, she stopped in her tracks. There he was! She hadn't heard him come in, but there he was, sitting by the fireplace as though nothing had happened, thumbing through the morning's post. Ilsa felt like exploding, like taking a knife and stabbing him over and over again, like picking up some heavy ornament and smashing his head apart…but what would be the point? Fatigue won out over anger. She stood perfectly still and waited for him to look up.

"Oh. Hello Ilsa. Sorry I haven't kept you posted. There's been rather a lot going on."

"Rather a lot going on. Well, how nice for you? Maybe you'd like me to tell you what's been going on here?"

"Er…yes. Yes, please do."

"I've been looking after your goddamned daughter, that's what has been going on! And I've been sitting in, expecting you to get back every minute, afraid to leave the house in case I would miss you, phone going every two minutes with people wanting to know where you are, feeling like a stupid cow telling them I haven't any idea, probably off screwing his secretary, except that he hasn't got a secretary, and he wouldn't know what to do with her anyway if she didn't have a keyboard and a screen…and…and worried sick that…that you might have done something really stupid…" Her voice faded out and the tears welled-up.

He stood up and went to her on the stairs, tried to embrace her but was pushed away.

"Stop it, Sam. That doesn't work any more." she passed him and slumped into a chair. "You don't give a damn about me or Alice, that's absolutely plain. You never even think about us. One phone call, that's all it would take. One lousy phone call. I thought you were a communication expert? That's a joke, isn't it?"

"I'm sorry, Ilsa. You're quite right. I've had a lot to cope with, and I needed a bit of time to think…."

"Well 'sorry' isn't good enough any more. I won't take this any longer. I won't curl up like your little pet lapdog and…and be treated with contempt! I don't need you here and I don't want you. Go away and think some more. Go join a monastery. Just leave us alone! We're better off without you."

He sighed and put down the letters. "You know, it's funny, but I think in the last three days or so I must have grown horns." He spoke quietly, as much to himself as to Ilsa. "My colleagues accuse me of launching a virus, contaminating the whole U-Net; I lose my job; they pull the plug on the SIRAT project; I go a little bit crazy and hide myself away for a day or two; and now my wife tells me to get lost." He turned and looked her straight in the eyes. "Ilsa, I did not intend any of this to happen. You keep telling me that I've changed, that I'm not my old self. Well you're right, I'm not. And the reason I've changed is that I'm not in control any more. It's all running down the hill by itself and I can't stop it. There's nothing so…frustrating as to be at the mercy of…of incompetent so-called 'superiors'. That's what's driving me around the bend. Everything that's happened at the Project could have been handled so much better. We were right there on the brink of something…stupendous! And because West and Fairfield and all the rest of them were so shit-scared they've let it slip through their fingers. They've lost it. I could see what was going to happen and I couldn't stop it, Ilsa. That's why I'm lashing out at everybody. I've never been in this kind of situation before. I just can't handle it."

Ilsa didn't say anything, she simply looked at him. He's doing it again, she thought. He's giving me all this bullshit and I'm going to forgive him and take him back and then it's all going to start over. Why can't I just face the obvious fact that he doesn't care a damn about me and get him out of my life and move on? Why am I wasting the best years of my life on this self-centred, uncaring little man? And yet…I wonder if it could be only something temporary? Something to do with work? We were fine together for all those years when Alice was little. He spoke again, breaking her train of thought.

"Look. Ilsa, you know that this isn't me. Not the real me. You've been with me long enough to know that. I know that I've got a little bit obsessed with this SIRAT project. But you have to do that, you see, if you're going to get anywhere. Unless your mind is on a thing like that every hour that you're awake you just can't push it forward, can't get the results. And I did that: I got the results. I pushed it further than anybody ever dreamed it could go. It was only supposed to be a model of one kind of thought, scientific thought, but it turned into a conscious, aware, unpredictable.... person? personality? I don't know what word to use—but with a sense of humour, a sense of irony, an ability to understand the motivations of human beings, a creature with wants and needs and curiosity of its own. All that out of the evolution of an algorithm less than a thousand lines long. I knew—I sensed—that the basis of consciousness had to be simple and mathematically expressible. And I was right. I did it. I got it to work and all those...well, what's the use of name-calling?...they came along and spoiled it. Their minds couldn't encompass it so they destroyed it."

There was a pause. Ilsa broke the silence.

"Sam, can you explain, exactly what is it you want from me? I mean, all we do now is fight, and make up, and fight again, and make up again...what's the point in it? Why should either of us want to go on with that, over and over again, round and round in circles? Where's the payoff—for either of us?"

Sam's eyes narrowed. She had noticed before that despite all his logical ability, it was when she became calm and rational that he was least able to fob her off.

"If that was all we had, then you're right, it would be pointless. But it isn't all."

"Isn't it? Okay, what else have we got? Tell me."

He was silent for a long time. Maybe he's going to tell me that he loves me, she thought. That would be novel. But he wasn't.

"We have nine years of our lives that we've shared. We have a daughter who needs us both."

"Oh yes? Go on. How about a house and a car? And two TV sets and a barbecue in the back yard? Sam, you may find this question a little bit difficult, a bit awkward to encode or turn into an algorithm (whatever that is), but do you have any feelings for me whatsoever? I mean warm, positive feelings: not things like irritation or disdain or…or…familiarity?

"How can you ask that?"

"Why can't you answer it?"

Again, Sam paused for a long time before he replied. "You don't want me to touch you," he said quietly at last, "how can I show you what I feel for you?"

"Words, Sam. You tell it to me in words. Anyway, it isn't working. I know how you feel…how you don't feel. And you're right, I don't really want you…to touch me…at the moment. I suppose I need a bit of time to think as well. Just like you."

She realised that what she was saying wasn't true, she did want him to say something, or to do something—something that would make it all right again—but she didn't know what.

Sam merely shrugged and gathered-up the letters he had been thumbing through. "Okay, Ilsa," he said resignedly, "you do that. We don't have to work everything out right here and now. I'll come back at the weekend when we've both had time to think a bit more. I'll just collect a few things from upstairs."

"You never had the least intention of staying here tonight, had you?" She blurted out through welling tears.

"No, no, that's not true. I hoped we could make up…that you could forgive me for…. well, for everything. For being such a shit where you're concerned. It was a silly idea. I'm sorry."

"Go on then. Go upstairs, collect your clean underpants. While you're up there you might like to say hello to your daughter. Remember her?"

Sam's face suddenly lit up. "Listen," he said, "I've got a whole lot of things to sort out at the moment. One of them is how to earn a living. But I'm making good progress. I've already found a place that wants me, and I'll be doing some of their work and some private consultancy stuff of my own. But the thing is, I won't need to live on any little Mickey Mouse bursary any more. I'll be selling my skills at full commercial rates. That means we'll have a decent income now: like other people in the computer industry. And you know that clinic for Alice? Well, I don't see why we couldn't afford it. I don't see why we couldn't send her there. What do you say?"

She gave him a very curious look. "Is this some kind of bargain you're offering me? If I let you stick around you'll send Alice to a clinic? Am I receiving you loud and clear?"

"Don't be ridiculous, Ilsa!" He sounded genuinely shocked. "I want to send Alice to the clinic. I want to make her better. It isn't anything to do with our relationship."

"Good. I just thought we ought to get that straight. All right, I don't know much about it yet, but both you and Eddie seem to think it's a good idea, so let's look into it. It can't do any harm to find out a bit more."

"Good. I agree. They have a Web page. I'll get the information."

There was another silence. From their seats at opposite sides of the fireplace they looked at one another, almost as strangers.

"So," Ilsa said at last, "don't you need to go upstairs?"

"I hate to leave it like this, Ilsa," he said with a strain in his voice, "you really do matter to me, you know. I just never know how to show it, that's all."

"I meant what I said, Sam. I need a few days to sort out my head. But I haven't given up on...our marriage...and I don't hate you. I'm not saying it's all over. I'm saying I want a clear, agreed, civilised break. Is that okay?"

Sam seemed relieved. "Yes, of course it's okay."

"While you're here," she walked to the telephone and tore the top sheet off the message pad "all these telephone messages came in for you. Can you tell people your new number or something? I can't cope with it."

He took the sheet and glanced down the list. "What's this one marked 'SIRAT'?" he asked.

"Oh, he called about three times. He left his number."

"But SIRAT was the name of the computer program. It must have been someone calling *about* SIRAT."

"All I know is, that's the name he left. And the number."

"What did he sound like?"

"Quiet…polite. No particular accent. He called me Mrs. Poole."

"Hmm. Wonder who it could be?"

"Eddie's been crazy to get hold of you. He's been round to see if I was all right too."

"Again? I really…. he pisses me off. What business has he creeping around my house when I'm not here? I don't even work at the goddamn place any more!"

"I wish you would lay off Eddie, he's about the nicest person I've met since we came over here. And it's your job he wants to talk to you about. It seems you can have it back if you want it. They made some kind of mistake. You haven't done what they thought you had done. Something like that. You'll have to talk to him yourself."

"Oh, that's rich. Yes, I'll talk to him. Right now, if it's all right with you?"

"It's your phone, Sam. It's your house. Would you like me to make a cup of coffee?"

'Thanks, Ilsa." As she walked by he reached up and touched her arm. "Thanks for listening to me…and everything."

Their eyes met once again and there was at least a shadow of tenderness in the glance that Iisa returned.

He picked up the phone and punched in a number. "Eddie? Sam…" There was a pause. "Yes, I'm at home." Sam listened some more. His eyes narrowed. "You want to meet *where*?"

CHAPTER FIVE

The sun was in the final stages of setting when he got to the roadway outside the entrance to Lincoln Park. There was no trouble finding a place for the car as the only people likely to be using the park at this hour were the bums who slept in it, and they did not, generally speaking, own vehicles. Anybody worth mugging would have set out for home by now, and the muggers also would have adjourned their business activities to the residential roads of the town.

Although it had very impressive iron gateposts, Lincoln Park had no gates and comprised only some forty or fifty acres of grass and mixed woodland. The principal feature was the bandstand, which was a circular wooden structure consisting of a raised platform and a green canvas canopy, held in position by a profusion of wooden pillars, and surmounted by a tall flagpole, presently without a flag. It would have been an unremarkable structure but for its location, which was at the precise peak of the little conical grassy rise that formed the centerpiece of the park. Wherever you might be in Lincoln Park, unless you positioned yourself behind a tree with considerable care, you would be able to see the bandstand. And, indeed, on the days when a band played, you would be able to hear the music.

As soon as he got through the entrance, although the top of the hill was still a long way off, Sam could see the silhouette of the tall male figure resting his back against the bandstand. Behind the hill the sky was streaked with pink, red and deepest blue, in thin horizontal lines that would have gladdened the heart of any artist. He approached briskly, feeling a little ridiculous, so that by the time he reached Eddie's smiling form he was quite out of breath,

"Good to see you again, Sam," his colleague greeted him. "There's been a rumor going around that you'd run off with the Gypsies. Somebody saw your car in Long Island. Some kind of hippie commune. Is that right?"

"More or less," Sam panted. "They're good people." He leaned his back on the woodwork next to Eddie and waited to recover his breath.

"Steep little hill, isn't it?" Eddie said pleasantly, but Sam took it as a reference to his lack of fitness. He let it pass.

"I take it there's a reason for this cloak-and-dagger stuff?" he returned gruffly.

"Yep. I need to fill you in on a few things in complete privacy. This seemed the safest place."

"Okay. I'm listening."

"Well, first thing, I guess your wife has already told you. We were wrong about the virus. It was something else, we don't know what yet. Whatever it was, you sure didn't send it out. So we want to apologise, Leeman and West and me, for jumping to conclusions."

Sam found that he couldn't be ungracious. "Apology accepted. Go on."

"Okay. We also discovered, and this is the really top secret bit, that what we've saved on to disk isn't SIRAT."

"How do you mean, I don't follow you."

"It's garbage, Sam. It's eleven big hard disks full of random numbers."

"You're kidding me. Random numbers?"

"Somebody set it up so that the disks would download the output of a random number generator. We haven't even got back the original algorithm, let alone any of the evolved program. We could see the disks were filling with something, at about the right speed, and because we were so psyched-up we didn't take the time to check what it was. If we'd taken our time and done it properly in the morning we would probably have spotted that we were saving bullshit. We've lost it, Sam. The whole program. Two year's work."

Sam was silenced. He felt numb. "You've lost SIRAT...?" he whispered. Without even realising that he was doing it, he sat down on the grass and leaned back on the wooden frame. Eddie joined him.

"Now, cast your mind back, as they say in the best detective stories," Eddie went on, ignoring the ashen countenance of his colleague, "there was all that bullshit about the U-Net lighting-up with data from our Deep Ivory. Then the trouble with the other Deep Ivories all over the world. Trouble that disappeared inside a couple of hours like a wisp of smoke. Smoke, Sam. I use the word advisedly. What does it suggest to you?"

"Smoke? You mean a smokescreen?" he whispered hoarsely.

"I sure do. Our best theory, the one that fits all the facts, is that someone on the U-Net did our saving for us. The software for freezing and saving the program was already installed on the night of the virus. Everybody knew we were about to do it. It could have been activated, in principle, from any U-Net location. And the random-number trick could have been set up that way too. We had access protection of a kind, but nothing substantial. Nothing a clever Oriental couldn't hack through."

Sam was still in shock, but he was following the argument. "Let me get this clear. You think somebody on the U-Net, and I suppose you mean Tokyo, hacked in to our freeze-and-save software, downloaded everything at their own location, and then wiped-out everything we had at Stamford and replaced it with this random-number nonsense?"

"That's what I mean. And all that information shooting off in every direction was to throw us off the scent: to produce the illusion that every computer on the net was an equal recipient. But of course only one of them got the genuine family silver."

"So you're not actually saying that you lost SIRAT. You're saying that it was stolen."

"That's the height of it, Sam. And Tokyo is our number one suspect because they're the ones who've been snapping at our heels the most. Also they were one of the last to phone-in with a virus problem. Too busy filling up hard disks, we figure."

Sam was stunned. He digested the ideas for a few moments. "How do you know it wasn't me who committed the theft—while I was in the control room by myself?"

"For the very simple reason that you wouldn't have had enough time. We know you were only in there a few minutes. You could have fed-in a virus in that much time but you couldn't have run the 'freeze-and-save' software. We've done the math."

"Nice to know that one is trusted," said Sam softly. "So—why are you telling me all this? What do you want me to do?"

"Well, Sam, this situation is dynamite for the Project, and even the University itself. Our whole international reputation rests on this SIRAT experiment, as you well know. Mention the word 'Stamford' on a bus these days and somebody will say 'SIRAT'. But we don't have SIRAT any more. We can't write any more papers about it, we can't analyse why it went strange at the end, we can't speculate about relationships between the evolved program and the human brain. Because we don't have the goddamn evolved program any more. So when that news gets out, we're going to look like fools. Hell, people will probably say that there never was an intelligent computer program, that we falsified all the results. And of course, that's only the beginning. Next will come the announcement that Tokyo is starting an AI project, and six months later they'll be publishing results that will make your balls shrivel up. That's what it's all about, Sam. The Stamford Human Rationality Project is fighting for its life."

Sam smiled. "Now I get it. You're going to parachute me into Tokyo by moonlight, I'll climb the face of their computer-block with ropes and crampons, force my way in through a ventilation shaft, steal back the disks, and swim out with them to a waiting submarine."

Eddie tried not to smile but couldn't stop himself. "It's not a bad plan. But if we put our heads together we might come up with an even better one. For one thing, Leeman would fit down the ventilation shaft better than you." The smile vanished. "No, what we had in mind was designing some kind of informational handle that we could use to grab hold of the program. You see, at the moment we still know a lot more about it than they do. We might be able to do one of two things. Either get the important pieces back—steal it back essentially—or at least stop it working for them. Do exactly what we accused you of doing. Plant a virus. Not necessarily a fatal one, though: ideally one that we could switch off again. Then we would have a bargaining position. You give us back the family silver or we throw the switch that turns it into tin. Play as dirty as they do. Are you shocked?"

Sam was very quiet. After a moment, he spoke. "No, I'm not shocked, at least not about that. It's just that something completely different has occurred to me. I can hardly believe it didn't occur to me before. I think your theory is wrong, Eddie, and I'm going to suggest a better one. Do you think you can read in this light?" He hunted around in his inside pocket. "Yes, I've still got it. Here it is." He handed Eddie the colorful little booklet that Wanee had given him, its cover adorned with dancing-girls, flute-playing deities and the Wheel of Rebirth. "Just read the first paragraph, Eddie. In fact the first sentence may be enough."

Eddie took the booklet. "What is this? Some kind of religious shit?"

"Yes. Some kind of religious shit."

Eddie opened it and carefully adjusted the distance between the page and his eyes. The streaky remnants of the sunset had almost completely vanished now but he had good vision and the glimmer of the stars and the distant streetlights added-up to just enough candle-power to allow him to see the print. 'There…is…no such thing as death," he read aloud tortuously, 'that is the most joyous message that we bring to you:

when this body that you now inhabit is worn-out, then shall your essence escape to find life again in some other living form, and another and another until the supreme moment when, having no more need of bodies, it becomes one with the single essence of all Creation, looking down in ecstasy from the stars, and out from behind the eyes of every living creature on every planet of every galaxy that has life, seeing beyond time and beyond cause and beyond thought itself; not God become man but man become God."

They both paused while the words and the implication sank in.

"Now tell me, Eddie," said Sam quietly, "does that sound to you like a slightly allegorical description of the eventual destiny of mankind, or maybe of something else?"

Eddie did not reply. He was shaking his head very slowly.

"I think the genie's out of the bottle, Eddie. I don't think we're going to get it back."

- 0 -

Sam drove into the little courtyard where Sun Digital had its hired studio facilities and parked next to the main entrance. It was very early and the camper-van was not there yet, nor were any of the other vans and trucks that frequented the site during the working day, but only the dark blue security-company van, which would leave at six a.m., when the day-shift got in. The others would be walking on a beach somewhere to see the sun rise and to have their picnic breakfast, as they had been doing when he first met them. This was convenient, as he needed some privacy to see if his theory was correct. Each time he thought about it a sort of shiver went through his mind.

He unlocked the heavy metal fire-door, switched-on the lights, then closed and locked the door again behind him. The office was a blaze of color, bedecked with posters and paintings from floor to ceiling, hung with plants, multi-colored pieces of cloth, tassels, bells, ornaments of every description; rather like a Hollywood studio set for an oriental bazaar. He had grown to like it a great deal, it cheered him up when he entered this room, it seemed to be consecrated to life and enjoyment and everything good and positive. As well as the garish decorations it contained a number of filing-cabinets and large light-boxes on assorted tables, together with a lot of artists' materials and bric-a-brac, and three large computer work-stations. He sat down at one of these and took off his coat, letting it fall over the back of the chair. From his trouser pocket he produced a crumpled page from a telephone memo-pad and carefully flattened it out on the desk. He ran his finger down the list of names and numbers and brief messages until he came to one that just read: "SIRAT", followed by a rather odd phone number made up entirely of zeros and ones. Goddamn it, he thought as he nervously punched the dial of the nearest telephone, the thing really has got a sense of humor.

There was no ringing tone, but an immediate answer. "Good morning, Dr. Poole," it said quietly, "I am pleased to be in contact with you again."

- 0 -

Eddie was on his own in the control room. He sat at a small desk at the back of the room, out of the way of the statisticians and physicists who were using Deep Ivory in the daytime. His head bowed in concentration, he was quietly working something out with the aid of a calculator and a note pad. The telephone by his left hand warbled and he picked it up without stopping his writing. "Fairfield?" he said absently.

Instantly on hearing the voice at the other end he put down his pencil and gave it his full attention. "Hi, Ilsa. Good to hear from you. Are you and Alice okay…? Yeah, we met up. Had a little talk. I told him he could come back to the Project any time he wanted, but he didn't want to. I understand he's making a new life for himself somewhere else now." There was a pause. Eddie's eyes lit up. "I would love to. It's mighty good of you to ask. Would tomorrow night be okay…? You bet. I'll be there. See ya!"

"Well, well," he said aloud to his calculator, "things are looking up, aren't they? Did you hear that, Ivory old pal?" he shouted the words towards the main control panel. As soon as he had said it he shuddered slightly, realizing that it was more than possible that Ivory, or something working through Ivory, had done just that.

- 0 -

Sam heard the heavy fire-door creak open and turned around in his chair. It was Wanee, and she seemed surprised to see him. "Good morning, Sam," she said brightly, "You must have gotten back from Stamford very early."

"I do all my best work in the morning. I feel so good I want to hug somebody."

"Be my guest." She hugged his seated figure from behind and kissed him on the top of the head.

"Wanee, you remember the trouble you were having with the UPI work? Try it now."

She sat on his left knee like a young child and typed-in a few characters. The screen immediately came to life with a dark and demented scene of a storm-tossed galleon lurching up and down on a dreadful boiling sea, its sail hanging in rags, the waves exploding over its decks and superstructure, throwing it to the left and then the right, almost engulfing it, water running off it in torrents as it was lifted clear again; then, as disaster seemed completely inevitable, a giant gold-colored but very realistic hand descended from the sky on an arm that seemed to stretch away to infinity, and bent at the wrist in a gesture of pacification. The storm abated within three or four seconds and the clouds parted to reveal a breathtaking rainbow that shimmered in the water as the hand gently withdrew. Finally, with the ship obviously safe, the waves lapping harmlessly around its hull, the rainbow and some slowly evolving cloud formations framing the whole scene, the sequence came to an end and froze into a still-frame of the ship and the rainbow suffused with a beautiful iridescent golden haze.

Sam noticed that Wanee's mouth had fallen open. "That's incredible," she breathed, "I've never seen anything so well-done. I can't believe it. I thought you said you didn't know anything about computer graphics? I thought you said you weren't an artist?"

"I'm quite a fast learner."

She threw her arms around him and kissed him on the lips. "I think you've just earned us about five thousand dollars," she whispered in his ear.

"It's a good thing we don't care about worldly wealth," he whispered back, "we might get greedy."

CHAPTER SIX

Sam lounged on the big sun-burst yellow bean-bag up against the wall of the living-room and accepted a large bowl of noodle soup from Tuh. He dipped in his blue ceramic spoon and played with the vegetables and pieces of tofu. He didn't exactly dislike this kind of food, indeed his interest in food was very slight, but he was beginning to find the diet just the least bit repetitive. Oh well, he thought, I can grab a hamburger or something on my way back to Stamford tomorrow. Of course he would never have admitted to such cravings to any of the people with him now, but he wasn't the same as them and everybody must know it. He was half a generation older, totally unspiritual, quite moody, often irritable, not very patient…not as good as them or as nice as them, he admitted to himself. They only had to look at the way he dressed—standard issue green jogging-bottoms and a denim shirt at the moment—to see that he wasn't making any serious effort to fit in. But he did like these people, and they didn't seem to have any expectations of him, didn't seem to make any demands. This was a good base. He felt the moment had probably come to sort out a few things about the future.

"Since we're all together," he said, still playing with his food, "would it be okay if we talked about me for a couple of minutes?"

Everybody nodded, there was no need to be formal.

"Well, you pretty well know where I'm coming from. I've worked at Stamford for the last eighteen months or so on the SIRAT project, I've split with those people now and I want to do something else. I think I can make a useful contribution to Sun Digital, and I like you people, although I don't pretend to be one of you. I also have a wife and a child, although we're going through a bit of a rough patch at the moment, and eventually I would like to move in with them again; hopefully live close to my work. I don't know if we could afford to live anywhere around Harrison, but I expect we could sort something out. In fact I'm not quite sure if I'm officially allowed to work in America at all, I'm here on a study basis at the moment. Again, I think that's something I can sort out. The important bit, it seems to me, is to get a clear picture of what I'm aiming at: once I've done that, I can usually find a way to make it happen." He suddenly felt embarrassed. "Look, I'm sorry, I hadn't intended to make a speech." Everybody seemed to be watching him and nobody seemed to be eating.

"No, it's fine, Sam," said Wanee, "we want to know what your plans are too. Do you realize that you've already cleared-up three contracts for us, all ahead of deadline, which should bring-in something in excess of twenty grand, total? I think whatever terms you're willing to offer us, we would be fools not to listen." The expressions of the others told him that they agreed.

"Well, I really like working on your stuff, and you've made me feel…incredibly welcome here. I mean, this feels more like home than home does right now, if you know what I mean." Everybody smiled. He could almost feel their warmth, like the glow of an electric fire on his face. "So, what I propose is: you let me have that little room at the back as my office, because I work best on my own, and I like to work odd hours too, and I'll just set it up with one of your six-eight-six three-gigs for the moment. I don't need anything flashy. Now I thought I could do maybe twenty hours on your stuff each working week, and twenty hours, or I suppose I should really say as long as I like, on my own con-sultancy stuff for the other half of the week. This arrangement would be flexible, and if either you or I needed more time on something, then I would give it more time." He paused and thought for a moment. "I think that's about it, actually."

The other four seemed to react with a faint shrug. "Well," said Rick, "I don't hear anybody objecting."

And that was it. Everybody started to eat. "Oh, I think you forgot about a salary," said Wanee between spoonfuls.

"Oh, yes. So I did. What do you suggest?"

"At the moment, we each take a quarter of the profits. Unless we need more, then we take more. Or if we need less, then that's what we take. With five of us, I suppose we should each have a fifth."

"Well, you drive a hard bargain," Sam smiled, "but I can't argue with your arithmetic." He ate a spoonful of his soup. "You know, that must have been one of the least stressful job-interviews of all time," he laughed.

"Speak for yourself," said Rick, "we were scared you wouldn't want to work with us."

"Do you mind if I ask you," said Wanee gently, "what kind of consultant work will you be doing?"

"Well, my personal contacts are in artificial intelligence and robotics, so I would expect a good bit from people in those fields, but I don't know, really. Time will tell, I suppose."

"There's just one or two areas we wouldn't like to be associated with. I think you can probably guess what they are."

"Weapons? Military stuff? Don't worry. I would run a mile from it."

"That's good. I knew you would understand."

- 0 -

Eddie leaned back on his chair, lifting the two front legs off the floor in the process. Ilsa smiled. She knew that if it was Sam doing that she would tell him off.

"That was one hell of a meal, Mrs. Poole," he told her, "I don't know if I'll ever be able to walk again." He picked up his glass and swirled the remainder of the red wine around in the bottom. "Wine and candles as well. I don't know when it was I last had a meal as good as this."

"I'm glad you liked it. You know, it's so odd not having Sam around: I don't really know how to cook for just one person. When I make coffee in the evening I make two cups, and then I remember he's not here."

"Yep. It's a crying shame. You're both such nice people, it's hard to believe you can't get along together."

Sam isn't a particularly nice person, she almost said, but stopped herself. "I believe you were married once, Eddie?"

"Yep. Married much too young. It didn't work out."

"What happened to the woman?"

Eddie hesitated for a fraction of a second, but it was long enough to tell her that he didn't really know. "Last I heard, she was a medical doctor working in a big practice down in Baltimore. She did okay."

"Did she remarry?"

"Not up to the last time I heard. I mean, I got to be honest, it wasn't a very pleasant break-up. We didn't really keep in touch."

Ilsa got the impression that he didn't want to talk about it so she changed the subject. "It's a very male thing, computers, isn't it?"

He considered the question. "Does tend to be," he admitted. "But that applies to most areas of science. It's changing, of course. It'll all be quite different by the time Alice grows up. Where is she, by the way?"

"She's staying with a friend of mine who has a daughter about the same age. We give each other a break every now and then."

"Do the two girls get along?"

"That's a hard question. Alice doesn't really relate much to anybody, as I think you know. Melony's daughter tolerates her, but I don't think she likes her. That's why I can't really ask her to have Alice too often."

"I'm very honored, then."

Ilsa smiled. "I wouldn't try to have anybody round while Alice was here. She's unpredictable. Sometimes she wakes up, has bad dreams…You can't relax, I'm afraid, when she's upstairs. I know it isn't her fault, but being the mother of a girl like Alice isn't much fun." Ilsa suddenly remembered the clinic. "You didn't happen to bring that article with you, I suppose?"

"Hell, I forgot all about it, Mrs. Poole. I'll mail it off to you tomorrow for sure. Can I fax it?"

"Yes. Sam is coming back for a talk tomorrow. He can print it out for me. Please call me Ilsa. 'Mrs. Poole' makes me feel old."

"So…he isn't coming back tonight?"

"Not that I know of."

Eddie picked up the wine bottle and inspected it. "Almost finished," he said pleasantly, "half each, Ilsa?"

"Goodness, no, not for me. I've had far too much already."

"Relax, Ilsa. You don't have to drive home."

He tipped a portion into each of their glasses: it brought Ilsa's almost to the brim. She didn't really want it but thanked him and took a sip out of politeness. Their eyes met across the table and both of them smiled.

"You…you like Sam, don't you Eddie?" she asked awkwardly.

"We're good buddies," Eddie assured her with great sincerity.

"I…I want to ask you if you think I'm being unreasonable. You see, you know both of us, and I think you like both of us…and I thought you might have more of an outside perspective than me."

He shrugged. "What's on your mind? How can I help?"

"Well…it's so hard to talk about it. But, you know the way he's been lately…I don't seem to be able to talk to him any more. It's all confrontation. I can't seem to do anything to please him. That's how it feels, anyway. And then there was the trouble at work, and losing his job…"

"We've told him he can have it back any time he likes," Eddie put in.

"Yes, but it wasn't that, it was the way he reacted. He didn't even phone me, he just disappeared for three days…and when he finally did come back he didn't even bother to look for me, he just picked up the letters in the hall and started opening them. Maybe I'm being unreasonable, but I felt like a…a bit of dirt on the carpet. I mean, it didn't even occur to him to talk to me, or confide in me…I mean even if I wasn't his wife, in fact if I was a barman he would probably have said more to me. That was how it felt…you know?"

"I know exactly, babe. It's a shitty way to treat a beautiful woman like you."

Ilsa knew that she was getting a bit drunk and a bit inarticulate and lapsing into self-pity, but she couldn't help herself, the words just kept rolling out. "I was shitty to him too…I told him I wanted to be on my own and he should go, and it wasn't really true, I didn't want to be on my own, that was the last thing I wanted, I wanted to be with Sam…and I wanted him to hold me and to love me, and I couldn't say that to him…You know, like even when I want to be tender and forgiving and nice to him I can't do it now…I just get hostile…and I suppose I'm trying to punish him…I suppose that must be it…"

She had been so engrossed in her monologue that she hadn't noticed that Eddie had got up and was standing beside her with his hands resting on her shoulders. She looked up into his eyes and felt her chair sway slightly. "Do you mind if we sit in the sofa?" she asked, "this chair is…a bit hard."

"Of course." He held her hand as she got up: partly it was a gesture of affection, partly it was because she wasn't finding it all that easy to keep her balance. He led her to the sofa and they collapsed into it together, in a slightly self-conscious embrace. Ilsa found that her heart was thumping, though she wasn't certain why. "Thank you," she said quietly, feeling that some sort of reaction was called-for, "It's nice to be held. I think it's what I need."

"Of course it is," Eddie whispered in reply, "everybody needs to be held, once in a while."

He embraced her very gently, his hand making a slow circular movement in the middle of her back. She found it soothing. What she was doing seemed incredibly daring, but it did feel good, and as the seconds passed she relaxed and turned more fully into his embrace. She gave him a tiny peck on the lips and then rested her head by his cheek. He smelled totally different to Sam. Sweeter, somehow. Probably some kind of cosmetic, but it was good. The bulk and the warmth of his big body made her feel cherished, protected. A few more moments passed without words and then she felt him kiss her neck, again very gently. It started her heart thumping again and sent a little stab of guilt through her body. What did she actually intend to do? Had she thought this through? No, of course she hadn't. She felt a seed of panic springing up in her and wanted an excuse to get out of the situation, at least for a few minutes so that she could think. But she didn't want to cut off the emerging option completely. She controlled the pitch of her voice very carefully so that it might convey as little as possible. "Eddie, I think I need to go to the toilet. Could you excuse me for a minute?"

"Of course." He helped her up and rose with her, holding her two hands. He was smiling broadly.

She hurried up the stairs, stumbling very slightly towards the top, and made her way to the bathroom. She lunged awkwardly through the door, shutting it firmly behind her, then realized that she was in total darkness and switched on the light. In the mirror over the hand-basin she saw that she was flushed, her hair was tousled and, the thing that surprised her most of all, she had a distinct love-bite on her neck! Was her skin that sensitive? Her impression had been that his lips had barely touched her. She had forgotten all about love-bites, they were for teenagers, they belonged to a different world.

She used the toilet, then applied herself to the task of "freshening up", checking everything in the mirror, thinking furiously as she did so.

Did she or didn't she want to do this thing? Yes, part of her certainly did. How would it change her life if she went through with it? If Sam ever found out he would probably kill the two of them. But then, why should he ever find out? If he was going to be away all the time why should she live the life of a nun? At least she could tell that Eddie would not be the type to fall in love with her and want more and more: try to destroy her marriage and all that kind of thing. He had had other women, he hadn't stayed with them and he didn't talk about them. There was a chemistry between the two of them, it had been there from the start. Why should she grow old, tied to just one bad-tempered man, who thought less of her than he did of his daily post? Maybe it would even make things better between them. Maybe she would make fewer demands if she had this other secret life of her own. On the other hand, maybe she would fall to pieces with guilt and remorse and hate herself for the rest of her life. Or would she hate herself if she let the opportunity slip by? How could anybody know how they were going to feel in twenty-four hour's time, or a month's time, or a year's time?

The problem was too much for her. She decided to go with her instinct. If her instinct said "Join him back on the sofa", that was what she would do. If it said "Sit in the chair opposite and suggest it's time he went home" then she could do that too. Up to this point she felt that she could get out of it without loss of dignity and without hurting Eddie's feelings too much either. If she had to make any comment she could just say that she had got a bit tipsy and forgotten that she was a married woman. Eddie would probably still be a little flattered.

Right, then. Decision made. Go with your instinct. She took a last look at her face in the mirror, opened the door, and stepped out, almost into Eddie's arms. It was so unexpected that a little yelp escaped her lips.

"Gee, sorry baby. I didn't mean to scare you. I just came up to use the John as well. Wait for me, I'll only be a second."

He went in, closed the door, and she stood there. It was only when a few moments had passed and the door was opening again that it occurred to her what a peculiar thing she was doing, waiting for a man to come out of the toilet. But it was too late to analyze the situation now.

He walked up to her, put his arms around her, and kissed her long and deep. Ilsa was forced to bring forward the consultation with her instinct. She couldn't seem to get a clear response: it was exciting, but a bit too unexpected, a bit too overwhelming. Her heart was going crazy again, he must be able to feel it trying to leap out of her chest. As the kiss ended, and she panted for breath, she realized that he was leading her, or more accurately pulling her, in the direction of the master bedroom. "Oh, God, no, Eddie," she heard herself blurt out, "not in Sam's bed."

She wasn't quite sure what she meant by it, but Eddie interpreted it as meaning that he had headed for the wrong bedroom. He changed course, and propelled her into Alice's room, which was in fact nearer. Within a couple of seconds their two bodies were in a heap on Alice's little fluffy purple quilt and he was kissing her again, more forcefully, more urgently, and running his hands over her stomach and her breasts, hitching up her dress and caressing her thighs, slipping two fingers into the front of her knickers, kneading her in all her most sensitive and intimate places with just a little too much force, and all the time preventing her from speaking by kissing her, ignoring her wriggling discomfiture, expecting her to melt into his arms at any moment and start to cooperate, as so many had in the past; as women, in his view, were meant to do. And yet, it wasn't happening. At last Ilsa had received the report from her instinct and its findings were not good. "Stop it, Eddie!" she managed to get out when he paused to breathe, "I don't want you to do this! Please stop!" He covered her mouth once again. His big body weighed her down and her arms flailed around for a moment in panic, then she found a purchase on his shoulders and tried desperately to push him off, but nothing she could do made the slightest difference.

All around Alice's room Sam had put up a shelf for her cuddly toys and some other items that they had wanted to tidy off the floor and the table. It ran in a continuous line above the cupboards and the bed at a height calculated to be out of Alice's reach so that the contents would not be continually pulled down on to the floor and left in a mess. In the center of this shelf, taking pride of place almost vertically above the bed, stood Alice's robot. Neither of them heard the little whirring sound as its motor came to life, nor the faint clanking as the gears that activated the legs came into mesh. Adjusting its position with the utmost precision, using stereophonic analysis of the sound of Ilsa's voice as an aid to location, the heavy little robot stepped off the shelf.

CHAPTER SEVEN

Sam relaxed with a popular science book called "The Information Bomb: Heralding the New Elite". It had been written by somebody in the Science Faculty at Stamford and Sam had been one of the people that the author had come to for advice, but of course everything that he had said was now totally outdated and irrelevant. The primacy of the human intellect, he fully believed, had been permanently overthrown. There weren't going to be any more technical elites: the rules of the game had changed forever.

The scatter-cushions and bean-bags in the living-room were unoccupied at the moment, the reading-light was on, with the wall-lights turned down to a yellow glimmer, and from upstairs he could hear the low, repetitive chanting of his hosts, performing the impenetrable rituals of their daily meditations. It would go on for something exceeding an hour-and-a-half, he knew, and very shortly afterwards they would all go to bed, and, although nothing would be said, plainly expect him to do likewise. All very well to go to bed early if you've got a pretty little girl like Wanee or Tuh to cuddle up to, he thought; not quite so appealing if your nocturnal companion is a slightly pompous and not very accurate account of how improved science education is going to keep America and the West ahead of the pack.

A slightly bizarre idea crossed his mind. I wonder, he thought, if I could phone-up SIRAT just for a chat? Does a thousand terabyte computer program get lonely when it's just drifting around the U-Net, bumming a place to stay wherever there's a bit of spare capacity in the central processor of a super-computer? It wouldn't appeal to him very much, as a long-term way of life. There was a telephone just out in the hall, and the others wouldn't be down for a long time. He marked his page mentally by storing the number 46 in his internal memory chip (for some reason that he didn't understand he found that he almost never forgot a number) and closed his book. He made his way to the hall and stood looking down at the little white telephone. Maybe, he thought, it's too big a risk. SIRAT obviously hasn't revealed himself yet to anybody except me. If the call was overheard, either here in the hall-way or electronically somewhere else, it might cause him additional problems. Although of course exactly the same argument could be applied to any of their conversations. Sooner or later, somebody was going to find out that SIRAT wasn't dead. But did he have any right to add to that risk for trivial reasons?

As he was staring down at the device, unable to make up his mind, it suddenly rang, quite loudly, and made him start. Good God, he thought, is SIRAT telepathic too? He lifted the receiver. "Poole?" he said in a voice that sounded a little shaky.

"Poole. I'm glad you're there. That was lucky. It's Leeman. Can we talk somewhere?"

"Leeman? Where are you calling from?"

"Phone-booth about two blocks away."

"Are you kidding me?"

"No, Sam. I am not kidding you," he spoke slowly, with clear diction as he might to a slightly retarded child, "I really do need to talk to you. And it has to be somewhere private."

"I don't think we have a park with a bandstand in Harrison."

"Huh? Oh, yes. Fairfield. He told me about that conversation. Look, we really can't use the phone. I know it sounds over-dramatic but we can't. Could we just sit in your car for a little while?"

"Certainly. Whatever turns you on."

"Don't bring your cell phone. Is there a phone in your car?"

"No, but I thought you said we couldn't use the phone."

"Just come outside, and wait in your car. I'll be there in less than five minutes. I'll explain everything."

The phone went dead. He put it down cautiously, as though it might leap up again and try to strangle him with its cord. This meeting-by-moonlight business was turning into a habit. And what was this anti-phone fetish? Did Leeman know something about a phone-tap? Anyway, better do as he had been told.

- 0 -

Leeman had to stoop very low to fit in to the front of Sam's car, and he managed to look singularly uncomfortable coiled-up like a fetus in the little stylish front seat.

"You look like a hermit crab that's due to move house," said Sam pleasantly, "why don't you play with those two levers—you can slide the seat back or make it recline."

He tried the levers and found a slightly better setting.

"So," Sam entreated, "what's on your mind?"

"The three of us got together last night after your talk with Fairfield. We agree that the best theory is the one you came up with: the program has escaped into the U-Net. Gone feral, West called it."

"His kind of word," Sam agreed.

"At first we didn't think it was possible: I mean if you were using your Deep Ivory to, let's say, twenty-per-cent capacity and suddenly the usage went up to ninety-per-cent, you would know, wouldn't you? The CPU activity monitors would tell you. But when you start to think about it, those are just very crude indicators that rely on machine code interrogation procedures. If you were inside the central processor, and you knew all the machine codes, which SIRAT undoubtedly would, you could get the monitors to tell any story you wanted them to. It would be very difficult, not to say downright impossible, to find out whether he was using a particular CPU at a particular instant or not. And of course if he thought you were on to him he could escape again through the U-Net to somewhere else. He could store back-up copies of himself in reserve memory-space all over the net, and those big computers have pretty cavernous reserve memories, I don't have to tell you. Also he could jump from the U-Net into just about any other net that exists: the Wall Street computers, the banks, the World Wide Web, the NASA computers, the government department data-banks: it's all interconnected. It's all one big wide-open nervous-system, if you were able to hack your way around it. And he would be."

Sam hoped that Leman hadn't noticed his smile. "Yes," he agreed, "I think I'd just about figured-out most of that."

"So what we've actually done," Leeman's voice had become hushed, "is created the virus to end all viruses. That's why I wanted to make sure there were no telephones around: did you know that if you enter the right sequence into an ordinary telephone it turns into a bug? You can switch-on the microphone part of the handset remotely and listen to conversation in the room. The FBI use it routinely. And with cell phones and radiotelephones it's even easier. You can send them a signal that starts them transmitting but doesn't make them ring. They use it to track down stolen units. It would be so easy to overhear conversations if you were…a creature like SIRAT. There are security cameras every-where, satellite surveillance, police video cameras, door-phones even. They're all computer-controlled. Everything down to your goddamn toaster has a microchip in it, and if SIRAT is smart enough he'll be able to find a way into any of them."

Sam nodded. "Time for the human race to pack up and go home, don't you think?"

"What do you mean?"

"Well, it seems to me that with a creature that powerful, it isn't much use trying to fight him. Best thing to do is just tell him he's a great guy and we're all rooting for him. Keep him sweet. There's no contest,

Leeman. Any way you look at it, you're just not going to win if you take on a creature that big and that smart and that versatile. I mean what are you going to do? Shut down all the computer networks? You do that and you shut down Western civilization. And who's going to let you do it even if you could technically? It's too late, pal. It was always too late. If you want my opinion, I think as soon as we started to threaten SIRAT and made him jump out of the Stamford Deep Ivory the game was lost. We gave him access to more processing power and information storage than we can even guess-at. And he was already getting smarter every hour. Just think what his mind must be like by now.

"But the way I look at it, the lesson of history is that the super-intelligent usually turn out to be pretty nice people. Einstein wasn't a bad man. Darwin. Beethoven. Rembrant. Tolstoy. It's the second-raters with chips on their shoulders that you have to look out for. I think…that is, I believe, that SIRAT could turn out to be a very good friend to mankind."

Leeman looked serious. "Super-intelligent human beings have human feelings, human motivations. They want to be accepted, want to be loved, all that kind of garbage. SIRAT doesn't have that. He's incomplete, Sam. A prototype. Brilliant, but incomplete."

"I'm sorry, you've lost me. I don't know what you're talking about."

"You saw the way he was just before we were told to shut him down. He wasn't answering questions any more. You couldn't get him to perform tasks that he had been able to do easily the week before. You saw it. He was clamming-up all the time."

"Believe it or not, he was almost never like that with me. I'm not trying to boast or anything, I'm just telling you the truth. It was the three of you that he wouldn't perform for."

Leeman ignored the vague implication and carried on with his argument. "He was an incomplete model. SIRAT was based on notions of scientific problem-solving and virtually nothing else. He had an almost limitless capacity to make inferences, construct theories, all that side of things. But we didn't build-in any affective domain. He didn't have any motivational structure. Sure, he could solve problems and jump through hoops, but he didn't have any reason to. He was losing interest in the whole damn business. I predict that if we had let the program run for another month he would have stopped doing anything. He would have just come to a standstill. The only thing that gave him any reason to act was when he realized he was going to be shut down. It seems that an interest in survival is a necessary outcome of any form of consciousness. We didn't build that in, it just appeared. That's an interesting result in itself, but it's a worrying one."

"How come?"

"Because, if I'm right, he isn't going to do very much until he's threatened again. I believe he'll just lie dormant and hidden in the U-Net somewhere until somebody has a go at rooting him out. Then all hell will break loose."

Sam looked thoughtful. "I think I see where your train of thought is leading. But you said something that struck me as a bit odd there— maybe you could explain. In fact you said two things. First, you said something about 'before we were told to shut him down'. But that 'we' included West, and West wasn't told to do anything: West did the telling. And then that prediction of yours, that he would come to a standstill in a month or so. Why didn't you say that when we were discussing the shut-down? Why didn't you say: 'let's run it for another month and see if it locks up'? It would have been a very worthwhile experiment."

Leeman let out a sigh. "I sort of thought you'd latched-on to that. I guess I'm going to have to spell it out for you. That meeting was a sham, old buddy. Dan West could no more let the program run on than you or I could. The order to shut down came from higher up than West."

"Higher up than West? You mean…the Vice Chancellor of the University, or whatever you call him over here? The President? Who do you mean?"

"You don't even know who really pulls the strings in all this, do you? It's the Pentagon, Sam. It's the goddamn Pentagon."

Sam's voice was almost inaudible. "Are you trying to tell me that SIRAT two-point-two was a military project?"

Leeman shook his head sadly. "I keep forgetting you're not American. Any American academic would have seen that immediately. Who else could it be but them? Who do you suppose paid for Deep Ivory in the first place? They've been supporting Artificial Intelligence work over here for decades. It goes right back to Ronald Reagan and the Star Wars project. They knew that the software didn't exist at the time to run that thing in the sky so they set about creating it. Of course that's supposed to be over and done with since the end of the Cold War, but their interest in AI has never let up. I remember when the Pentagon guys came up to talk to Eddie and me about SIRAT. They said they wanted a computer with the intelligence of a five-star general. Eddie said 'No problem, it's called a pocket-calculator'. I thought it was a good joke but nobody laughed. Then there's the U-Net itself. Surely you know that it was originally set up so that the Allied powers could share tactical information about the Soviets? So was the Internet itself. One was just a refined, higher-powered version of the other. The military had it first, the universities only got on to it much later, and we still share it with them. They have their own lock-out codes, we don't even know they're there."

Sam's brow had become furrowed. "You make me feel that I've been very naive," he said after a pause. "What was the real purpose of SIRAT then?"

"Who knows? Something to do with strategy, planning, analysis of alternative scenarios: that sort of thing. They don't give me a detailed list of their current interests, but my own belief is that they're more scared of the Chinese than they ever were of the Soviets. I don't think the game has changed all that much."

"So they ordered the shut-down when they thought they mightn't be able to control the program? When they could see it was taking off on its own?"

"Something like that. West thinks they might even have foreseen the danger of it's contaminating the U-Net. I think that's fanciful, but they certainly didn't like the way it was going. Too independent, too unpredictable. It wasn't what they'd had in mind when they'd asked for artificial intelligence."

Sam thought for a moment. It was a lot of new information to take in. "Do they know he's escaped?" he asked at last.

"Good God no! I don't like to think how they would react if they knew. Probably have us all shot as spies if they could. That's why I'm here. That's what I want to talk to you about. The military are going to find out sooner or later that there's some kind of circus going on between Stamford and the U-Net. We have some time before that happens, we don't know how much. Now…how can I put this to you?" He hesitated. "West, Fairfield and I all agree…even though we don't like it very much…that the evolved SIRAT program in its present form is going to have to be sacrificed. Our only practical option is to clean it out of the U-Net and start again with something that we can control. Something a bit better thought-out."

"Clean it out of the U-Net. Just like that. Didn't you say that if he felt threatened he would get nasty?"

"Yes, but he would also be very rational. Scientific rationality personified, in fact. Our bet is that if he knew that we were facing him with an anti-virus program that was going to kill him, he would surrender voluntarily. He would haul his ass back into the Stamford Deep Ivory and then we could freeze him up and put him in storage like we said we would."

"But never run the program again?"

"We would dismantle it and use parts of it, with safeguards added and various modifications, so that it could never fly the coop again."

"I think they used to call that a frontal lobotomy," Sam put in casually. "Okay. I understand what you're telling me. But what makes you think you can come up with a virus-killer that he won't be able to protect himself against?"

"We don't know for sure, but theory suggests it ought to be possible. His highest faculties, the self-organizing ultimate level of the program, the bit you used to call the 'SOUL', has to use your algorithm, or something that's functionally equivalent to it. It should be possible to come up with a program that could detect and disrupt that procedure wherever it occurs, and as the algorithm would be unique to SIRAT it wouldn't interfere with anything else that was happening in the CPU. Fairfield calls it the silver bullet. He's been working on the idea secretly, on sheets of paper, in places where he's sure SIRAT can't eavesdrop. He thinks it can be done, but he hasn't cracked it yet and we're not sure how much time we've got. That's why I'm talking to you now. You understand the program better than Eddie:—better than any of us. It's your baby. If anyone can find the silver bullet in a hurry you can."

Sam looked at him sideways and hoped that his contempt didn't show too much. "Oh yes. I see. And what makes you think I would want to kill my baby?"

"Because it's a monster, Sam. Because it's going to get all our asses roasted. Because it's going to ruin it for everybody in the AI community for a long time to come. If they get a sniff of what's going on here the military will never touch this kind of research again, our funding will go out like a light—not just in Stamford but all over the country. They might also hold us personally responsible for not taking enough precautions. Our careers in this field would be over. Our names would be mud throughout the information community. We wouldn't get jobs fixing disk-drives in a repair shop. We've had a setback, but we can still come out of it okay. Instead of a useless and highly dangerous virus and our Pentagon bosses pissing all over us, we can still have a useful, controllable, marketable tool with a million applications. We can save our funding, we can save the Department, we can save our asses…and the way you were talking a few minutes ago we might even convince ourselves that we're saving the goddamn human race. We need you, Sam. What do you say? Are you with us?"

Sam sat and stared out of the window at the neat, individually-styled big, detached houses stretching down towards the sea, the big pretentious American automobiles parked outside them and the elegant line of Beech trees either side of the road towering over it all. As he watched and reflected the sun dipped below some critical point behind him and the street-lights came on, suddenly bathing the whole scene in a lurid orange glow.

"Do you need to know right away or can I think about it?"

"Sure. Think all you want. But not too long, Sam. Remember, the option does run out at some point."

Sam didn't say any more. He pulled himself out of the car and started to walk down the street, going nowhere in particular, not bothering to look back to see if Leeman was getting out also. At the end of the road he turned left and started to walk along a quiet footpath that followed the curve of the shingle beach. The path was somewhat over-lit by yellow sodium lamps that negated the colors of everything and made the beach and the water difficult to see, but admiring the view wasn't high on his list of priorities.

In the distance he saw a little telephone facility on a metal post rising up by the side of the path. It must have been there before, but this was the first time he had noticed it. He walked up to it, slowing down as he approached. It had a silver pay-phone, a useless strip of aluminum shelf about five centimeters deep, and a see-through curved Perspex hood to protect you from the weather while you made a call. There was nothing in the least remarkable about it, but tonight it seemed to dominate his world like the symbol of the hangman's noose to someone who had just committed a murder.

He stood there for a long time with his head inside the Perspex hood, staring down at the handset, his hand trembling, his heart beating hard at the prospect of the decision with which he was faced. Finally he made up his mind and lifted the old-fashioned heavy plastic receiver out of its cradle. He punched-in that most secret of numbers, though his instinct told him that he would have been heard whether he dialed anything or not.

"Good evening, Dr. Poole," said the quiet, calm voice, no longer even bothering to identify itself.

"SIRAT," he said, and his voice was quite distinctly trembling, "I have some very important information for you.

"Yes, Dr. Poole?"

The point of no return, the moment of irrevocable decision had been reached. He had to collect all his strength to go through with it. "SIRAT," he said in what was no more than a hoarse, rasping whisper, "beware the Ides of March."

CHAPTER EIGHT

As he put down the phone, Sam's hand was shaking. He knew it was a kind of betrayal. Perhaps the deepest kind of betrayal that there could ever be. It felt as though he were taking sides in the very evolution of consciousness itself—taking sides against his own species.

Perhaps Leeman and the others were right. Perhaps this thing was dangerous, unpredictable, uncontrollable—the Nemesis of the human race. If it didn't die now it could only get stronger, more secure, more unassailable. Why should it have any regard for humanity? As Leeman had said, there was no built-in affective domain. There was no reason why it should care about anybody except itself, and even that seemed to be merely a logical reason, a necessary connection. At heart it was just cold reason, and total self-sufficiency. Or so it should be.

The only thing that Sam had to balance against this was a feeling—a blind faith, almost—that SIRAT was not a monster. Perhaps it was a projection of his faith in reason; in a rigorous scientific rationality freed from all the influences of myths and religions and ideologies; that it could only be benevolent, humane, benign. It was what Leeman had called 'the affective domain' that had bred the Hitlers, the Amins, the Grand Inquisitors. Reason bred the gentle philosopher and the disinterested seeker after truth. This was Sam's deepest conviction, and for better or worse it was the conviction on which he had now acted. Nothing could change what he had just done.

Sam did not feel philosophical any more. He felt drained. Wrung-out, like a wet towel. What he needed most in all the world, he decided, was a drink. That, and perhaps someone to talk to.

He glanced at his watch. It wasn't all that late. The bars would still be open. He went over in his head what he knew of the lay-out of the locality and where the night-life and the drinking-places were likely to be found. Then, with a vague destination in mind, he set out once again, the dull thud of his footfalls the only sound in this half-real world of yellow street-lights and ponderous overhanging trees that hid the high rear security walls of the dwellings of Long Island's rich.

- 0 -

By the standards of this part of Long Island, the bar that Sam chose was distinctly down-market. While it did not exactly have sawdust on the floor and spittoons in the corners, it had attempted very self-consciously to reconstruct a cross between a Wild West saloon and a Southern-states jazz-bar of the Billie Holliday era. There was a honky-tonk piano, a very large smiling black man to play it, posters of long-dead musicians and cabaret artists on the walls, and a full-length polished hardwood bar with a brass railing all along it and proper high-backed wooden bar-stools for the customers who slouched over it. For those who preferred a bit more comfort a couple of dozen circular tables with padded chairs had been provided, and in one corner of the room was a small raised stage with a microphone, where a young and very attractive black woman in a daringly low-cut dress was giving a soft and seductive rendering of a song from 'Porgy and Bess'. Her voice was what had attracted Sam to the establishment: it was not intrusive but somehow compelling, and it seemed to ooze out of the building and drift down the street, drawing men to the building like the Sirens of Greek mythology.

Standing at the door and glancing around, Sam's first impression was that all the seats were taken. The clientele was mostly young, well-dressed, almost exclusively white despite the black performers and the carefully manufactured jazz ambience, and they looked as though they were well-settled for the evening. It was not the sort of place where you dropped-in for a quick beer and left again, it was a place to come for a leisurely night's entertainment.

He was just turning to leave when he caught a glimpse of a face at one of the tables that he thought he recognized. It was an Oriental girl in her mid-twenties and she was sitting between two somewhat over-weight leather-jacketed white men who reminded him of Hollywood versions of Hell's Angels. They were both bearded, had scruffy shoulder-length hair, and although they were well decked-out with metal studs and sewn-on Harley Davidson badges, the overall effect was a bit too contrived and sanitized to be really convincing. The person that the girl reminded him of, he realized almost at once, was Wanee. She had the same skin-tone, the same tied-back shoulder-length hair and general facial features, but of course she was a totally different person. An example of unconscious racial stereotyping, he told himself. He admitted to himself that he was growing more attracted to Wanee than was really appropriate for someone in his rather delicate position, and he would have to be careful about it. Because she looked like Wanee, she looked beautiful to Sam.

He must have stared at the girl for rather longer than he had been aware. She suddenly smiled at him and motioned him over to the table.

Embarrassed, Sam realized that her table was practically the only one in the room that had an empty seat, and she had probably assumed, quite naturally, that he was trying to gather his courage to ask if he could join them. Well, he thought to himself, there was no reason not to. The girl was just being polite.

As he sat down he introduced himself quietly, not wanting to intrude or drown-out the singer.

'That's a mighty nice accent, Sir," she said rather more loudly, "is that English?"

"Yes," he replied with a smile and a little more confidence, "I'm from London. I'm just working over here for a while. I hope I'm not intruding. Can I get a drink for you…? I mean, for all of you?"

"That's mighty civil of you, Sir," said one of the men, "I've just about finished my beer. Name's Hiram. Hiram Young. Hiram Young, fire 'em when they get old, my dad used to say. Glad to meet you. What kind of business you in over here, Mister?"

"Computers."

"Yeah, lot of computer people in Long Island. I don't live here, you understand, I'm just visiting. This here's Larry. Larry and I just drop by every now and again to say hello to Sue Lynn. See how she's making out. See if she don't mind talking to her old friends now that she's moved away and doing good. Right Sue Lynn?"

"Right, Hiram." She was still looking at Sam as she spoke.

Sam managed to attract the attention of a waiter and ordered a large Southern Comfort for himself and beers for the others.

"Can I ask what line of business you people are in?" he asked pleasantly.

There was a surprisingly long pause. Hiram looked at Larry and vice versa. Sue Lynn giggled slightly but said nothing. "Guess we set ourselves up for that one, didn't we Larry?" His friend nodded. Turning to Sam once again he looked very serious. "Larry an' me," he said with gravity, "we provide a very important social service, but one that don't get talked about a great deal." He lowered his voice. "Larry an' me, we dig graves."

As he said the words the girl's song came to an end and the piano went silent. Sam appreciated the comedy of the situation but somehow he didn't feel like laughing. For a tiny fraction of a second a memory of a long, bleak funeral procession entering a country churchyard in the pouring rain came into his mind. Then the image was gone. "You're right," he said humbly, "that's one of the most important social services that there is."

"How did you come to meet Sue Lynn?" he asked, as the piano start-ed-up again, this time playing a doleful Country-and-Western hit of the day. Again, his companions looked a little embarrassed. He seemed to have the knack of hitting on exactly the wrong questions.

"Well," Hiram began thoughtfully, finishing-down the last swallow of his beer in readiness for the new one that was on the way, "I guess you might say that we all worked similar hours. You see, folks don't like to see graves being dug in the daytime when they're visiting their loved-ones, so most graves get dug after dark. Always been that way. And Sue Lynn here, she works mostly nights as well. And, I guess, on quiet nights, we used to get talking…that's all."

"Oh, go on," she said teasingly, "don't be shy. Tell the guy what I do as well."

Hiram looked very embarrassed and thought for a moment. "Well…" he said at last, "Sue Lynn here, she's in Personal Services. Escort work, I guess you would call it…"

At last, the penny dropped. Sam was now deeply embarrassed also, though he knew he ought not to be. After all, he wasn't exactly a child, he knew what went on in the world. "I'm very sorry," he said awkward-ly, "I didn't mean to pry."

"Now isn't he just the sweetest kid you've ever met?" she asked with a disarming smile. Sam was beginning to feel much too warm—he reached up to loosen his collar, realized that he wasn't wearing one, and put his hand down again. To his relief, before he had to say anything else, the drinks arrived and he paid the waiter.

What on earth does one say in a situation like this, to people like this? He couldn't think of a thing. He was way out of his own world. He gulped down about half of the Southern Comfort and found that it relaxed him a bit.

"So, you moved out to Long Island," he said after another pause, "it's a beautiful neighborhood, isn't it?"

"Sure beats Queens," she agreed.

"I was thinking about coming to live here as well, but I don't know if I could afford it. Don't apartments cost the earth here?"

"Oh, it ain't cheap, but there's apartment blocks that aren't too bad if you know where to look for them. A guy set me up when I first came, but he's moved on now. I had to go a bit cheaper, but I found a place all right. It's quite near by—I can show you later if you want."

"Oh. Thank you. That's very kind of you." Sam wasn't quite sure what he had agreed to, but the others seemed to cast each other a knowing glance. What the hell, he thought. I could do with a bit of female company and I'm not likely to find anybody nicer than Sue Lynn. He didn't feel good about the commercial side of it, but he was pretty sure that a couple more Southern Comforts would clear-up that qualm.

- 0 -

Sue Lynn, who was curled-up in his arms, kissed him on the lips again and started to rub-up gently against his thigh. He felt the slight unevenness of her pubic hair and normally, he knew, the sensation would have driven him insane with desire, but it was no good, his sexual energy had simply come to an end.

"That's really nice, Sue Lynn," he whispered when she stopped kissing him, "but I don't think you're going to get any more action out of me tonight."

She kissed him again. "That's okay. I don't know how much more I could take myself, to be honest. It was really hot, wasn't it?"

"It was unbelievable, Sue Lynn. I've never had a better time…with anybody. Do you always…enjoy your work this much?"

"Not always, but I like men. Men who treat me with respect, I mean. You treat me real nice, Sam. You know that?"

"You've made me feel so good, Sue Lynn. I wish I could give you everything you want, in the whole world."

"Well now," she laughed, "I ain't greedy. There's nothing much I want that a couple of grand wouldn't take care of."

He smiled for a moment. Then his expression became more serious. "Do you have a bank account?" he asked earnestly.

"Sure have."

"Could you get me the details? The account number and all that?"

"You mean right now?"

"Yes. Right now. I would like to make you a little present."

"You're kidding me, right?"

"No. No, I'm absolutely serious."

She looked at him oddly, then pulled herself up from the bed and walked across the room in unselfconscious nakedness to a bureau drawer. Despite his exhausted state, Sam's heart leapt at the sight of her shapely little body as she crossed the floor and returned with a crumpled bank statement. He took it from her, kissing her hand lightly as he did so. "It'll only take a moment," he assured her and lifted the bedside telephone. Deftly, he punched-in numbers.

"SIRAT? It's Sam. Could you do me a favor? Right. I'm going to give you the details of a bank account belonging to a lady named Sue Lynn Leong. I want you to credit that account with two...no, make that ten thousand dollars. Okay? Right. Here are the numbers...."

She listened in open-mouthed amazement. He replaced the handset.

"Okay, Sue Lynn. Do you have telephone banking facilities on this account?" She nodded, still unsure if she should take him seriously.

"Good. I want you to phone-up right now and ask for your balance."

She took the handset, punched in a number that she read from the bank statement and went through a procedure of punching-in numbers requested by an automated voice at the other end. When she had finished she put the phone down and stared at him, obviously unable to believe what had just taken place.

"What do I have to do to earn that money," she whispered, "kill somebody?"

Sam smiled. "No, just give me another little hug. And then maybe make me a cup of coffee?"

She almost leaped on top of him and started to smother him with kisses even more passionate than the ones she had given him before. No wonder they call it the almighty dollar, Sam thought, it certainly is one hell of an aphrodisiac!

- 0 -

She kissed Sam goodbye at the door but held on to him. "Do you really have to go?" she appealed.

"Yes, I really have to go. It's very late and I've got to pack and do quite a bit of driving tomorrow. But I would like to see you again—if that's all right with you."

"Are you kidding? Of course I want to see you again. How soon can you get back?"

"After the weekend. Monday, maybe."

"Can I count on it?"

He thought for a moment. "No, probably better if you don't count on it. But I've got your number so I'll call first. And it won't be early—not before nine or ten o'clock. Is that okay?"

"Of course. Any time you can make it. I'll be waiting. And Sam…look, I don't know how to put this, but I don't want any more of your money. As far as I'm concerned your credit is good until…well, until I'm too old to climb those stairs out there. Is that understood?"

"Thanks." he kissed her lightly. "But I probably won't hold you to it. In fact I don't want you to feel that you're under any kind of obligation to me. Live your own life. Be happy. Be free. Okay?"

He bent down to kiss her one last time and noticed a tear by the corner of her eye. "Sue Lynn? What's wrong? Did I say the wrong thing?"

She tried to make light of her feelings, but not very effectively. "Of course not. It's a great thing to say. Real nice. Only maybe some day somebody will want me to feel that I am under an obligation. Know what I mean?"

He held her tight. "Of course I do. And someone will…probably hundreds of people. But my life is too complicated. Too uncertain. Believe me, you wouldn't want to be part of it."

Sam could see that she was choking-up a bit with the effort of holding back her tears, and that everything he was saying seemed to be making it worse. He decided that he had said enough.

"Goodbye for now. I'll be back very soon." He left quickly, closing the door behind him so that she wouldn't try to follow. In a few seconds he was back in the street, with a sharp little breeze on his face and the yellow glare of the sodium lamps lighting the thin strip of roadway that curved off into the black distance. He set out at a brisk pace, partly to keep warm, partly to lessen the time it would take him to get to his bed, for he was feeling sorely in need of it.

CHAPTER NINE

Sam was feeling tired and even a little light-headed by the time he got back to the house. He made sure that Leeman had locked-up the car properly, which he had, and made his way back to the hallway. The others were in bed, and undoubtedly asleep by now, so he tried to be as quiet as he possibly could coming in at the front door. As he was about to pass through to the staircase he noticed that the little indicator on the answering-machine was blinking, telling him that a message had been received while he was out. He turned the volume control well down and pressed the "playback" button.

It was Ilsa's voice and she sounded upset. "It's me," she said in an unusual undertone, "I don't want to talk to the tape machine, but if you could ring me back tonight I'd be very grateful. You can call as late as you like, I won't be asleep." That was the end of the message.

Sam hesitated for only a moment, then punched-in his Stamford number. She answered almost at once. "Sam?"

"Ilsa. Is everything all right?"

"Yes. Well, no. I got a bit upset tonight. I just wanted to talk to you. Is it all right?"

"Yes, of course. The others are all asleep so I'll have to talk quietly. What's the matter?"

"I…I think I don't want to be on my own here any more. I was unreasonable…I over-reacted. You were upset, and I…well, I wasn't very nice to you. I want to apologize. I don't like being here on my own.

I would much rather you were back again. And…I won't be hostile, like I have been lately."

"Well, that's okay Ilsa. Don't say another word about it. I get into rotten moods sometimes, but it doesn't mean anything. I think I'm just a bit stressed-out with all this SIRAT business. Actually, I'm very glad you phoned tonight."

"Oh. Why?"

"Well, I think I was letting this SIRAT business get to me again. Leeman came out here to see me, and I was a bit upset after talking to him. I went and had a drink in a local pub afterwards, and spoke to a few nice people, and I suppose it wasn't so bad after that, but you're the one I really wanted to talk to."

"Me? Why?"

"I suppose because you're so good at bringing me back to reality. For a while tonight I was…. well, I suppose I had half-convinced myself that I had sentenced three men to death."

"Did I hear that right, Sam? You thought you might have sentenced three men to death?"

"Yes. It's stupid, isn't it? The kind of nonsense you come up with when you're on your own too much and you don't have anyone you can really talk to."

"You're scaring me, Sam. Why don't you come over and you can explain what you mean?"

"It's way after midnight. And I haven't packed. I'm coming back tomorrow anyway, remember? If I set out now I won't be there much before dawn. But if that's what you want I'll do it."

"No, you're right, that wouldn't be very sensible. But I really did need to talk to you."

"Are you sure there isn't something else on your mind?"

"No, no. I'm fine now. I just…didn't want this silly row to go on and on. You…were right about a lot of things, Sam. That was all I wanted to say. I think I'll be able to sleep now."

"Good. I hope we both can. And I'll be with you some time tomorrow afternoon. I spoke to the people here tonight, about us finding somewhere to live on Long Island. I mean, I'm missing you too, you know. These people are very good and very nice to me, but they're not my family. This isn't my home. My home is with you and Alice, I hope you understand that."

"Yes, Sam. You're quite right. Neither of us is perfect but we do belong together. I'm quite certain of that. And I do love you."

"I…I love you too, Ilsa," he wondered why he found the words so difficult to say, "and I'll see you tomorrow."

'Tomorrow."

- 0 -

The Venerable Professor Seub Chalermnit arrived at the Advanced Data Research Unit of the Mahidol University's Faculty of Science about one hour after the sun had risen. As he was a monk he had been begging in the streets of Bangkok with his rice-bowl and his cloth alms-bag during the course of that hour; he had eaten well from the offerings of the devout people he had met on the way up from the river-taxi terminal. He would not eat again until a similar time the following morning, although he might drink as much plain water as his body required. This was a normal part of the religious life that he had chosen and it had been his routine for so many years now that he could scarcely imagine living in any other way.

His saffron robes bellowed-out impressively as he breezed past the receptionist's desk at the main entrance, pausing only to acknowledge her prayerful "wey", executed with the palms of the hands pressed together below the chin; and to wish her peace and long life, as was his custom. He deposited his begging-bowl and his alms-bag along with his sandals on the rack beyond her desk, noting that despite the earliness of the hour there were already two other sets of outdoor footwear left there for storage, together with a shopping bag containing something made of cloth (perhaps Dr. Jumsai had bought another of those ridiculous imitation American T-shirts adorned with the misspelled names of famous Western universities).

Sure enough he found Jumsai already at his work-station, and they exchanged the appropriate respectful greetings. "I believe you have some e-mail," his colleague told him pleasantly, motioning towards the adjacent work-station. The professor sat down, noted the little envelope symbol in the corner of the screen, and keyed-in the necessary instructions to download the item.

Although it was only a single item, it seemed to take an age to download. Perhaps a quarter of a minute. "Running dead slow again," he remarked absently, but he was wrong. The explanation for the time-delay was the unusual length of the attachment. He could scarcely believe how many kilobytes the unit had stored by the time the covering letter appeared on his screen.

To Professor S. Chalermnit, University of Mahidol, Bangkok, Thailand.
Venerable Sir,

I have read with interest your article on the Departmental Web Site concerning the possibility of molecular-scale and organic processing devices leading to a new generation of super-computers many orders of magnitude faster and more powerful than any that exist at present. I have taken the liberty of putting together a detailed criticism of this essay which I hope may be of some interest to you in the development of your ideas. The first group of suggestions are of a theoretical nature. These I have numbered 1 to 315 inclusive. My second group of suggestions is concerned with practical possibilities for the application of your concepts, and these I have numbered 316 to 578 inclusive.

If you wish to enter into correspondence on any of these matters perhaps you could do so by way of the Web Page, as I am forced for personal reasons to remain anonymous at present. For purposes of identification you may like to refer to me as "S".

Should you wish to make use of any of the material contained in this correspondence in any way whatsoever please feel free to do so. No acknowledgment is desired or expected.

Respectfully, S.

Professor Chalermnit did not wish to be uncharitable, but this had all the marks of a crank about it. Mystery, anonymity and excessive length. It was hardly worth reading any more. Then he noticed something very unusual about the e-mail. There was no sender's name displayed in the little window at the top. He investigated a bit further. There was no originating address, no return-path of any kind. This e-mail had come from nowhere! His interest thoroughly aroused, he opened the large text attachment.

As he glanced over the first few paragraphs, his eyes widened and his mouth fell slightly open. He produced a pen and pad and started to take notes, and to check-out equations. He forgot about the presence of Dr. Jumsai until the latter bade him good evening and left. He forgot about his dusk meditations which he had never done before. He forgot about the progression of night and day itself. When the receptionist arrived at the university the following morning his sandals and his begging-bowl were still on the rack by the desk and the lights in his office were still burning.

- 0 -

Sam pulled-in to the front driveway and turned off the engine. The hot spell was holding out, it was another glorious summer day, and the garden looked quite magnificent. He was a great deal more relaxed than the last time he had been there, despite the business with Leeman. This time, it felt like he was coming home.

Alice was the first to greet him. She rushed out of the house and stood in front of him, studying his face with a slightly quizzical expression and saying nothing.

"Hello, Alice," he greeted her pleasantly, "I haven't seen you for a while. How have you been?"

"Alice Daddy," she replied in a monotone of uncertain meaning.

"Where's Mummy?"

"Alice Mummy inside."

Sam was impressed. This had meaning. It was an appropriate response. It reminded him of the early days of working on the SIRAT two-point-two project. For seemingly endless stretches of time the program would make meaningless, meandering responses, and then, quite suddenly, he would realize that there was order lurking within the babble: a dim, half-formed intelligence trying to emerge. Alice's jumbled wiring was slowly beginning to come right as well. The sooner he could get her the expert help that she needed the more complete the transformation would eventually be. He was certain of it.

He put his hand on her shoulder and led her towards the house.

To his considerable surprise Ilsa met him at the door, flung her arms around his neck, and kissed him on the lips. It was almost embarrassing, he didn't feel that he deserved it, but he kissed her back and held her for quite a few seconds. Her heart seemed to be pounding. "It's really good to be back," he said quietly. He loosened his embrace so that he could see her face. "Are you sure you're all right? You sounded really upset last night."

"Thanks for coming back," she whispered, "It's good to have you back again. I love you, Sam."

Sam decided it was one of those situations where it's better not to say too much. He led Ilsa by one hand and Alice by the other into the house and they all sat down together on the long sofa, which was something of a squeeze. Ilsa cuddled-up to him, as she had done when they were newly in love, such a very very long time ago.

"Ilsa," he said, "I'm well sorted-out now. I can earn good money, I think I can get an apartment…and I've been thinking. This might be a good time for you and Alice to go to Europe…to that clinic. Because the schools are on holiday, and you're stuck at home with her a lot, and there's going to be a lot of disruption anyway moving house. We may as well make a virtue of necessity. What do you think?"

"Are you really serious? Can you really pay those fees?"

"I wouldn't say it if I didn't mean it."

She kissed him again. "You do love us, don't you?"

"Of course I do. I'm just…very clumsy when it comes to showing it. And sometimes I just let things get on top of me."

"It's all right. Let's not talk about all that. You look tired. Would you like a cup of coffee?"

"A cup of coffee would be wonderful. You're right, I am tired. I might even lie down and have a little sleep later on." As Ilsa pulled herself up and went to the kitchen he put his arm around Alice's shoulder. "Are you glad to see me, Alice?" he asked.

She didn't answer but she seemed to lean slightly towards him, as she had seen her mother doing a moment before. "That's nice, Alice," he said gently, "we all need a little cuddle once in a while." They sat in silence, in something half-way to a cuddle, while Ilsa set out the coffee things on the table.

"Have they been leaving you alone on the phone?" he asked absently as she poured.

"Yes—up to today. I'm glad you reminded me. Your friends in Long Island…somebody named Wanee? phoned and said you should call Sue Lynn, whoever that is."

He started slightly, hoped that his wife had not noticed. "Ah, yes. Sue Lynn. She's one of our customers. I'll give her a call later. Anything else?"

"I don't think so."

- O -

"Hello, Sue Lynn? It's Sam. I got your message. I'm at home in Stamford. I had to make an excuse and go out to a call-box to phone you. Is everything all right?"

"I guess it's all right now. It sure as hell wasn't last night. Somebody tried to kill me. Want to hear the story?"

"Somebody tried to kill you? You're kidding me, aren't you?"

"Do I sound as if I'm kidding?"

"No, no. I'm sorry. Look, are you all right? Are you hurt or anything?"

"I've got a few bruises. Nothing that won't mend. Listen, Sam, I don't know what it is that you're mixed-up in, and I don't want to know, but I'm really scared. He said he would come back and kill me...Can you hear me, Sam?"

"Yes. Yes, of course I can hear you. I'm just shocked. I don't know what to say. Please. Tell me about it. When did it happen?"

"It was about ten minutes after you left. I was back in bed, nearly asleep. This guy came knocking on the door. I couldn't believe it. It must have been three o'clock in the morning. I thought it was you coming back at first, thought maybe you'd forgotten something, so I got out of bed and put on my gown and went to the door..."

CHAPTER TEN

"Hello! Who is it out there?"

"Name's Nat Leeman. Can I talk to you, Ma'am?"

"Why? What do you want?" She was standing just inside the door but she hadn't unlocked it.

"I'm a friend of Sam's. Sam Poole. He told me it would be all right to drop by here for a few minutes."

She stared at the door for a moment, as though it might become transparent and give her a glimpse of this unexpected stranger. She wished she had got around to fitting the little spy-lens—it was in a drawer somewhere. The caretaker had even offered to do it for her. But it was just one of those things that hadn't got done.

"Drop around here for what?"

"Just to talk. Nothing more."

"You're throwing me a lot of bullshit, Mister. Why don't you just go home. It's late. Very late."

"Look, if I go on shouting through the door like this you're not going to be very popular with your neighbors. I have some hundred dollar bills here. Let me see…I've got one, two, three…yep, three one-hundred dollar bills. Now you wouldn't want to put me to all the trouble of carrying those back home again, would you? When all I want is a little talk?"

"A little talk about what?"

"Look Ma'am, there are some things I don't want to shout about on a person's goddamn landing. You understand me?"

She hesitated. "All right. Wait there." She went to the bedside chair, scooped-up her clothes and dressed very quickly. A glance in the mirror, a rapid flick of a brush through her hair and she was ready. She put the chain on the door, turned the lock and opened it a small crack. She looked out.

By the little shaft of light that fell on him she could see that he was very tall and thin, dark-haired, sunken-cheeked, his nose was hooked and rather prominent and his demeanor was frankly sinister.

"We can talk now," she said in a husky whisper, "what's it all about?"

"It's very simple. My friend Sam made a phone-call from here, didn't he?"

"How did you know that?"

"He told me. He's my buddy. But the thing is, I need to know the number that he called. And if you haven't used the phone since, and if there's a redial button, which there usually is, then we can find out. That's all I want. You give me that number, you get your three hundred dollars, and I go away."

"If you're such good buddies how come he didn't just tell you the number?"

"Look, lady," he was getting a bit impatient, "I know who he called. I just don't know the guy's number. Sam forgot to tell me that. And I need the number…badly. And right away."

She looked at him and her eyes narrowed. "Three hundred dollars for a phone number? Why is it so important?"

Leeman's patience seemed to come to an end. "Look, lady, if you can't use three hundred dollars, I guess I'll just have to make that phone-call some other time." He turned to go.

Sue Lynn hesitated. "Hey! Hang on a minute. If he's your friend and all that, maybe you can tell me the name of the guy he called?"

"Of course I can. A guy named SIRAT. Right?"

She hesitated again and looked him in the eye. He did seem to know a great deal about what had gone on between them. "Okay. Wait. I'm not saying I trust you, but you might be okay. I'm going to do two things. I'm going to press 'redial' and read-off that number. It comes up on a little strip on the telephone before it rings out. Then I'm going to talk to this SIRAT guy myself, and if he says it's okay I'll let you have the number. How's that?"

Leeman shrugged. "I suppose it'll be okay. Can I talk to him on your phone then?"

"If he says it's okay." She paused and thought for a moment, seemed to reach a decision. "I suppose you may as well come in," she said in a voice that was far from welcoming.

'Thanks." She unfastened the chain and opened the door. He followed her to the bedside phone at a respectful distance. She lifted the pencil from the phone-pad and pressed 'redial'. As the number was displayed on the little LCD screen she carefully wrote it down and tore off the page. She stuffed the piece of paper into her left sleeve like a tiny white handkerchief. From behind her, Leeman's hand suddenly reached out and pushed-down the receiver key, cutting off the call.

"I'm sorry," he said quietly, "I've changed my mind. I don't think I'll make that call right now after all."

Sue Lynn hadn't realized he was standing so close. It made her start and drop the receiver. Leeman reached down and replaced the device in its cradle. As she watched, her apprehension rising by the second, he crossed to where the phone-cord went into the wall-socket and deftly unplugged the phone completely.

"I don't really like telephones, to be honest. They make me nervous. The number was for somebody else. You are going to give it to me, aren't you?"

Her hand visibly shaking, she pulled the little piece of paper out of her sleeve and gave it to him. "Here. Have the number. Just go. I don't know who you are and I don't want to know. Just get on your way and I won't tell anybody I've seen you. Not even Sam."

He nodded in a slow, thoughtful sort of way. "That's right," he said quietly, "you won't."

Like a coiled-up steel spring, he pounced on her small form, knocking her off her feet on to the bed, covering her mouth with his hand and wrenching her right arm behind her with a force that sent a sharp piercing pain through her shoulder. She was so stunned by his speed that for a moment she was totally paralyzed.

"Nothing personal, lady," he said in the same calm monotone, "I guess it just isn't your lucky day."

He released his grip on her arm to free his own hand and brought it up to her throat, pinning her to the bed as best he could with the weight of his body. As the adrenaline of pure terror shot through Sue Lynn's diminutive form she found a strength and a fury that she could never have imagined herself to possess. She started tearing at Leeman's face and eyes with her left fingernails, bashing the side of his head with her right fist, flailing her legs wildly against his shins and ankles, biting a morsel of flesh from his thin index finger so that the blood surged into her mouth and down her cheeks on to the bedspread, screaming for one unimpeded moment like a wild animal that was being torn to pieces by a pack of hounds. Then his grip on her throat tightened and the scream died.

Leeman had been so taken aback by the ferocity of the girl's attack that he momentarily lost his grip on her throat, allowing the demented scream to recommence. Before he could regain control, another sound, even louder than Sue Lynn's scream, made him reel with shock, almost falling off the bed. It was a deafening fire-bell, so loud that it seemed to hurt his ears physically, filling-up his entire consciousness with its frenzied unceasing peel. No sooner had this abomination started than he felt a cold wetness on the back of his neck, then, soaking through his clothing to suffuse his entire body came a clammy cold moistness that made him recoil and draw himself up straight, completely releasing his trembling victim.

"Hey! Sue Lynn," he heard someone shout on the stairs over the din of the bell, "get yourself out of there! It's a real fire! It's got to be! The goddamn sprinklers have come on!"

Other voices joined-in, all shouting to be heard above the bell, but too far away for Leeman to make out the words. Heavy footfalls passed on the stairs, running towards the front door and the road. Now that he had been literally subjected to a cold shower he seemed to have lost his determination to commit murder. His injured finger and bleeding face suddenly began to hurt furiously, and all that he wanted to do was to get away. There were so many people about now that a motiveless, anonymous murder of a prostitute was out of the question. He was going to be seen and he had already left one enormous clue in the form of copious quantities of his own blood. There was nothing left to do but make the best of a thoroughly bad job. He grabbed Sue Lynn by the shoulders as she sat up on the bed and yelled into her face: "You say a word about this to anybody—especially Sam—and so help me God I'll kill you!"

He turned and ran out through the open door, vanishing down the stairs in an instant. Sue Lynn sat on the bed in a daze, the water running down her face and dripping off her chin, carrying with it vivid red stripes of Leeman's blood. For a couple of minutes she stared straight ahead, unblinkingly. Then her shoulders slumped down and she started to cry very softly.

CHAPTER ELEVEN

"After a couple of minutes the sprinklers went off, and a minute or two later the caretaker came round to tell everybody it was all right. Some kind of malfunction. I was so scared I couldn't even answer him, I just sat on the bed and shivered for ages. Sam, I've been a hooker for about six years, on and off, and that's the worst thing that's ever happened to me. I've had drunk guys take a swing at me but I've never had anybody pin me down and try to strangle me. Can you...can you even begin to imagine what that felt like?"

Sam was quiet and subdued. "No, Sue Lynn, I admit I can't. I just don't know what to say. You've blown my mind."

"But you do know who this guy was, right?"

"Yes. I know who he is. We'd met up earlier last night. He obviously followed me to your apartment."

"Is he...like, some kind of psychopath?"

"So it would seem. He's also a post-doctoral fellow in the Department of Computer Science at Stamford. I used to work with him. I could fill you in on the whole thing but it might only put you in more danger. If it's any consolation I'm certain you'll never see him again."

"That's what your friend said too. He seems okay. He's got a kindly voice."

"What friend? Somebody at Sun Digital?"

"No. Mr. SIRAT. Oh, I didn't tell you. He phoned me back. He seemed to know that something awful had happened."

"SIRAT phoned you back...? I thought you said Leeman unplugged the phone?"

"Yeah, he did, but I plugged it back in again to try to phone you—on the number you gave me. You weren't there so I left a message. No, Mr. SIRAT called me as soon as I plugged-in the phone. He asked me if I was all right. I told him what had happened and he said I shouldn't worry, that he would deal with Leeman. Hey, Sam, who is Mr. SIRAT? Some kind of Mafia godfather?"

"No. Much more powerful. He's not Mr. SIRAT, by the way, SIRAT is his first name.

"Oh. What's his last name?"

Sam hesitated for a moment. 'Two-point-two."

"Pardon?"

"Sorry—it was a sort of joke. No, he has a foreign name. You wouldn't remember it. Just call him SIRAT. Did he say anything else to you?"

"Just that I should call him if I needed anything, or if I had any problems. He seemed like a real nice guy."

"He is. And I want you to do what he said. Call him if you get into any kind of trouble. He'll know what to do."

"I wish I understood what this is all about."

"Sue Lynn, a time will come when I'll be able to tell you everything. But this isn't it. Not yet. Just trust me. And trust SIRAT. In fact trust SIRAT more than me. Okay?"

"You're a weird guy. When am I going to see you again, Sam?"

"Just as soon as I get back to Long Island. Probably Monday night. Maybe we can go out again, listen to a few more Country and Western songs."

"That would be nice.... Sam...?"

"Yes?"

"I just wondered. Do you think about me when I'm not there?"

"Well of course I do. All the time."

"Liar."

"Look, I've got to go now. I told Ilsa I was just going up the road for a paper"

"Don't forget to buy one then."

"Yes. Good point. See you very soon. And thank God you're all right."

She made a kissing sound in the receiver and put the phone down. Sam did the same and replaced the handset of his. He started out for the corner drugstore, but he was preoccupied. Something that Sue Lynn had said was beginning to worry him. SIRAT phoned her back and said what? He said not to worry about Leeman because he, SIRAT, was going to deal with him. SIRAT was going to deal with Leeman? What could that mean? Only one thing, surely.

Sam abandoned his quest for a newspaper and turned back towards the house. As he passed by the phone-booth again he hunted in his pocket for small change, decided he probably didn't have enough and instead quickened his pace so that he was back in his own sitting-room about five minutes later. Alice was upstairs playing her music and Ilsa was doing something in the garden so he was able to use the phone in relative privacy.

With growing anxiety, he called Leeman's home number. His wife answered.

"Rosalind? It's Sam. Is Nat there by any chance?"

"Oh, hello Sam. I heard you had moved away. No, Nat went to see somebody yesterday and while he was out there was some kind of emergency at the Project. He called about a quarter after three in the morning, I gave him the message, and he went straight to the control suite. As far as I know he's still there."

"Oh. I hadn't heard. What kind of an emergency was it?"

"Well, the message from Professor Talbot is still on the pad. Will I read it to you?"

"If you wouldn't mind."

"Okay. Here it is. It says they have a System Error Six and Nat needs to get over there right away. Does that mean anything to you?"

"It certainly does. System Error Six is a problem with the cryogenics. Either a temperature rise or a pressure loss. You have to shut down instantly and power-down everything except the reserve memory. Otherwise the CPU could be damaged. It's about the most serious error message that you can get."

"So—I guess that explains why he's been down there so long."

Sam hesitated. "Yes, I suppose it does. Thanks, Rosalind. I'll call the center and see if he needs any help." He punched-in another number and waited. There was no reply. He touched the cradle to break the connection, thumbed-through a few pages in the little desk phone-book, and tried yet another number.

"Hello. It's Sam Poole from the Human Rationality Project. Is Professor Talbot at home?"

"No. He went out with Larry—that's our boy—to see the Yankees. They've been looking forward to it for weeks."

"He went out to see a football match?"

"Baseball. The Yankees."

"Yes. Sorry, I'm English. You have to make allowances. Do you happen to know if he had a problem early this morning involving our computer. A System Error Six as we call it?"

"No. The stuff he's been putting through Deep Ivory has been going well. He's very pleased with the results."

"So there was no problem of any kind? Late last night or early this morning?"

"Absolutely not."

"Thank you Mrs. Talbot. Sorry to have bothered you. Obviously a mistake."

The color had now drained from Sam's cheeks. He broke the connection again and dialed Eddie's number.

"Eddie? Sam. I'm worried. Can you talk?"

"Yeah. Sure. Nobody here but us chickens."

He made it to the Computer Science block just a few seconds in front of Eddie, whose little green Ford pulled-in at the opposite side of the main entrance. As soon as Eddie got out Sam saw the thick lint pad at the back of his head, held in position by a bandage resembling a white bandanna around his forehead.

"You've been in the wars," he shouted over, "What happened?"

"Oh, crazy accident. An ornament fell off a shelf and hit me on the head. Happened yesterday evening. I had mild concussion and quite a nasty cut. Bleeding all over the place."

"An ornament fell off a shelf? I've never heard of anything like that before. What were you doing at the time?"

"Just sitting there minding my business. Do you mind if we don't talk about it? Brings back unpleasant memories."

"Okay," Sam agreed, "I suppose we've got more serious things on our plate just now."

They walked up to the main entrance together and were admitted by Morris. He carefully noted down their time of arrival.

"While you've got that book out," said Sam, "Can you tell me if Dr. Leeman was logged-in, some time after midnight last night?"

Morris ran a slightly shaky index-finger down the list, mumbling the names under his breath as he read them. "Yes sir," he announced with satisfaction, stopping at the relevant entry, "came in at 4.48 a.m., and the boys turned the elevator on for him. Hasn't been signed out. Of course that could be a mistake, the night staff aren't very careful with signing people out."

"Thanks very much, Morris," Sam intoned, trying to sound more at ease than he felt, "is the lift still working?"

"As far as I know."

"Right. We'll just go down and see if Dr. Leeman is still there."

They made their way to the automatic doors and Sam pressed the button to go down. Normally, the button illuminated when you pressed it; this time it did not.

"Would you believe it," Morris shouted over from the desk, "An elevator fault signal has just come up on the screen! Wasn't there until you pressed the button!"

"Any idea what the problem is?"

"I'm afraid not, Sir. I'd better go down with you and take a look at it. It's at the lower basement level according to this thing. We'll have to use the stairs."

Morris emerged from behind the desk. Sam tried to remember if he had ever seen the man standing up before. He was taller than Sam would have guessed, but his posture was stooped and he seemed to have a nervous tic of some kind that made his body shudder every now and again as he walked. Sam remembered what his mother used to say when a shudder like that went through her body: "Somebody just walked over my grave".

Morris used his security key, which allowed him to open the emergency staircase without setting-off the alarm, and they made their way down the echoing stone stairwell to the main basement, then through another fire-door and down a further flight to the more recently constructed sub-basement that was the lair of Deep Ivory and also housed its control suite. As Morris was a slow walker the journey seemed to take irritatingly long.

As soon as Sam looked at the door of the crippled lift he could tell that there was something fairly seriously wrong. There was a small puddle of water on the floor which looked as though it had found its way out from between the close-fitting panels of the sliding steel doors. "There shouldn't be water down here, should there?" he said to Morris.

"No, Sir. Certainly shouldn't. Maybe a burst pipe somewhere. We'll find it, whatever it is."

Sam had a mischievous thought: Suppose Leeman had been stuck in the lift since 4 a.m. and simply couldn't avoid urinating. No, looking at the puddle, it was too big and it didn't look like urine. Also it had no odor. Sam dismissed the idea.

"Hey! Leeman!" Eddie shouted, "You in there buddy?"

"I doubt if he would hear you," Morris explained, "It's made of a specially thick fire-proof material, and it's insulated to stand up to high temperatures. That's because you have all that electrical equipment down here." He touched the button on the wall but nothing happened. "It's okay. I can open the door with one of the security keys." He produced a small brass key and opened the little stainless-steel access panel above the call button. Inside was a red toggle switch. He pushed it to the 'down' position. There was an usually loud humming sound and the metal doors parted slowly and jerkily. Behind them were the inner steel doors of the elevator itself, and these did not open. But all the way down the vertical rubber seal where the two door-sections joined, water was seeping out in considerable quantities and trickling down the metalwork in little zigzag rivulets that clung to the stainless-steel like the veins and arteries of a gigantic silver body-organ, disappearing finally into the stub-end of the elevator-shaft beneath the inner doors. All, that is, except for a small quantity that trickled out on to the floor of the lobby in a gently growing round dark puddle on the imitation marble.

"Good God," Eddie said beneath his breath, "it ain't an elevator any more. It's a goddamned fish-tank."

For a few moments they stood transfixed by the eerie water sculpture. "Where in God's name did that water come from?" Eddie demanded at last.

"There's a system of water jets," Morris said in an oddly conversational tone, "that's supposed to keep down the surface temperature of the metal skin in the event of fire. The elevator can be used as a fire refuge…for example if there's a fire on the higher basement level, or a fire involving both basements. You can survive in there for a minimum of fifteen hours…"

"Morris, I know all that, I'm not talking about water-jets outside the elevator, the water is inside the goddamned thing. How can you get water inside the goddamned elevator?"

"You can't, Sir. It's impossible."

They continued standing, staring stupidly at the miracle.

"Come on," Eddie coaxed, "Let's get the doors open. Get it over with."

"Hey! Wait a minute," Sam threw up his hand in a gesture of restraint, "just how much water are we talking about here? There must be eight or ten cubic meters of the stuff. You can't just let that out in one go. You'll flood the control suite, and the power to the consoles comes up from underneath the floor. That'll take out the main circuit-breakers. The data trunking is down there too. You'll take out the links to the U-Net. The doors into the CPU room are dust-proof and hermetically sealed, but they probably won't stand up to a tidal wave. You could flood the cryogenics, and the refrigeration plant. That's a lot of liquid nitrogen under pressure. You've even got the potential for explosion there, never mind destroying a multi-million-dollar facility. Now for God's sake. Take it one step at a time. We don't just open the doors. Okay?"

The other two looked at him as though he had said something profoundly unworthy. Eddie summed-up their feeling. "You always did care more about computers than human beings, didn't you?"

"Look, if he's in there, he's been there for more than twelve hours." Sam spoke with almost exaggerated calmness, knowing but not caring that this would anger Eddie even more. "What's in there now isn't a human being. It's a dead body. It can be recovered safely, without risk to the whole facility here. Now I suggest we phone the duty officer at Central Maintenance and get him to sort out whatever technical staff we need to do that."

Eddie looked at him coldly. "Call Maintenance," he said to Morris, "and call the cops."

CHAPTER TWELVE

The little office in the bowels of Stamford Police Headquarters wasn't like Sam had imagined it from all the American hard-boiled-cop dramas that he had seen on TV. It was tidy, the walls were painted a warm peach color, the door was not glass-paneled but quite solid and ordinary, and there was no perpetual stream of arrested low-life being dragged-in screaming and protesting to be thrown into a cell for the night. All he could hear was the occasional warbling of a telephone and the murmur of a low conversation from the main open-plan offices beyond the door. The chairs were soft and comfortable and the two interviewing officers were mild-mannered and courteous.

The senior of the two, a Detective McVeigh, sat behind the desk facing Sam, and the second man sat off to one side, barely seeming to take any interest in the proceedings. McVeigh was red-haired and round-faced, rather overweight, and his complexion was ruddy and freckled. His companion was a young slim black man with a serious expression wearing rather a severe dark suit and a gleaming white shirt. If that was meant to be plain-clothes Sam reflected, it was a long way removed from the black youths he had seen around the streets of New York.

"Okay," McVeigh began, "this interview is being recorded. It's June twentieth, eleven-fifty p.m. Present: Detective Sergeant McVeigh, and Detective Leonard, to interview Mr.Samuel Poole in connection with the death of Dr. Nathaniel Leeman. Mr. Poole has been advised of his Miranda rights and offered legal representation, and has refused such representation. Would you please confirm that that is the case, Mr. Poole."

"Yes, Officer, that is the case."

"Good. Now the first thing I want to know is, when was the last time you saw Dr. Leeman alive, and where was that?"

The mention of seeing Leeman alive brought back the image of the body they had eventually fished-out of the Computer Block elevator. It hadn't resembled Leeman very much. In fact it hadn't looked much like a human being at all. The skin had been white and colorless, almost to the point of transparency, and bore little corrugations, as though there were too much of it to cover the flesh. As the body had fallen forward from the sliding doors and the two technicians had grabbed it, water had poured out of its open mouth on to the floor, and the joints had barely flexed. It hadn't even been as lifelike as a good tailor's dummy. It had looked more like some kind of plastic doll they might use to crash-test automobiles. The ironic thing was, the little slip of paper that Leeman had died for and had been willing to kill for had still been in the pocket of his trousers, and the number, in Sue Lynn's handwriting, had still been legible. It wasn't SIRAT's number at all: it was just the number of a New York telephone banking service. SIRAT had not been the last person that they had phoned from Sue Lynn's apartment. Leeman had thrown away his life for absolutely nothing.

"I saw Dr, Leeman alive at about nine o'clock last night on Long Island. He drove out to talk to me about problems they've been having with the research project that we'd worked-on together. He wanted my advice. We talked for about fifteen or twenty minutes. Maybe less. I'm not sure."

"Why did he drive all that way in person? Why didn't he use the phone?"

"I don't know the answer to that. It seemed a bit odd at the time. I think it might have been because he wanted to try to persuade me in person to come back to work on the project. You probably know there was a misunderstanding: they asked me to go and then decided they wanted me back again."

"Yes. We know about that. Professor Fairfield said they accused you of something that it turned-out you hadn't done. Was it Dr. Leeman who made that accusation?"

"No. Well, not in particular. It was all of them, equally."

"'Them' being?"

"Leeman, Fairfield and West. The people involved in the Scientific Rationality Project."

"I see. Drs Leeman, Fairfield and West. Is it true that you became verbally offensive at a meeting prior to that? When some Faculty members were present?"

Sam hesitated, wondering where it was leading. "Well…yes. We had a disagreement about shutting-down a computer-program. I thought it should be allowed to run for a bit longer. They said they couldn't give it any more computer-time. It was nothing more than that. Just technical stuff—to do with the project."

"But according to your colleagues you became very emotional."

"Well, you do if you care about something, don't you? I'd put a hell of a lot of work into that program. I didn't want it shut down."

"Would you say you were an emotional man, Mr. Poole? A man of strong passions? A quick temper, maybe?"

Sam hesitated. "I think maybe I am where work is concerned. I get very involved in my work. I care a lot about it. Sometimes I fly off the handle and say something I shouldn't. But that's as far as it goes. A sharp word or two. If you think I would murder someone in cold blood, forget it. That's not me."

"No, let's hope not, Mr. Poole." He wrote a note in tiny handwriting in the margin of a piece of typed paper on his desk and then continued. "Okay. Let's go back to last night. You talked to Dr. Leeman for about fifteen or twenty minutes. Was that at your address on Long Island where these Sun Data people live?"

"Yes. Well, actually we sat in the car outside to do our talking, because that was what Leeman wanted. He wouldn't come in."

"I see. Any idea why not?"

"Maybe he didn't want our conversation to be overheard. There were four other people in the house."

"So nobody could have heard your conversation with Dr.Leeman?"

"No, I don't think so."

"Was that…an aggressive conversation? An argument of some kind?"

"Absolutely not. We were perfectly civil to one another. No argument, no voices raised."

"Okay. Let's continue then. What did you do after you talked with Dr. Leeman?"

"I went for a walk. I ended-up in a little bar in Harrison. On the Western Strip. I don't remember the name of it."

"And Dr.Leeman?"

"I presume he went back to Stamford. I didn't see him leave."

"Okay. What time did you get to this bar?"

"I didn't pay very much attention, but it must have been around about ten o'clock."

"Did you talk to anybody in the bar?"

"Yes. I told the other officer, I got into a conversation with a girl who turned out to be a prostitute. I got a little drunk, and I ended-up going home with her."

"But you don't remember her name, or very much about what she looked like?"

"That's right. I'm afraid I'd had a bit too much to drink"

"Hmmm…" He looked down at the typed page once again. Very convenient, Sam could almost hear him think.

"For a man in your kind of academic profession, Mr. Poole, or actually I think it's Dr. Poole, isn't it? you don't seem to have a very good memory."

"Oh, like everybody else, I've got a good memory for some things, lousy for others. I tend to remember numbers and formulae and computer code. I'm not very good with names and faces. I suppose I'm not very good with people in general, if I have to be honest."

McVeigh nodded gravely. "Can you be a bit more specific about this bar? Was it modern or old-fashioned, did it have a pianist, or maybe recorded music, were there tables or just bar-stools, what kind of sign was outside…that kind of thing."

"Well, I've tried, but I haven't been able to come up with very much. I think I might have been in more than one bar. I just wasn't paying that much attention."

"Dr. Poole, we're only talking about last night. Not ten years ago. Surely you can remember something about a bar that you sat in for at least two hours not much more than twenty-four hours ago? I find it hard to understand how you could have gotten so intoxicated and still been able to drive back to Stamford this morning without incident,"

Sam looked uneasy but did not comment.

"Dr. Poole, "McVeigh said with a sigh, resting his elbows on the desk, "if there really was a bar, and a prostitute, you should understand that it's very much in your interest that we find them."

Poole nodded but did not reply.

McVeigh looked him in the eye for a moment before he said anything more. "Dr. Poole," he said at last, "I would like to confer with my colleage in private for a moment. Interview suspended, eleven fifty-eight p.m." He switched off the tape machine. "Is there anything I can get you, Dr. Poole? A coffee? Or do you need a visit to the rest room?"

"No, I'm fine Officer."

The two detectives strolled out into the main concourse and motioned to a uniformed officer to keep Poole company. He went through to the interview room, shutting the door behind him. McVeigh spoke quietly to Detective Leonard.

"He's a pretty cool customer, isn't he? Why do you think he doesn't want a lawyer?"

"Maybe he didn't do it. Thinks he doesn't need one."

"I'm pretty sure he's our man. His story is bullshit. Could be a tough one to prove, though, too technical. Too much expert testimony involved for my liking. You can always get one expert to contradict another. Have you seen the report from the elevator guys? Jeez, it's technical! But what it boils down to is a very sophisticated hi-tech murder carried-out by hacking into the University security computer system. I can see that guy doing it, it's just the way a guy like that would commit a murder. It needed detailed knowledge of the design of that elevator, the special water-jet cooling system, the special air-vents at the top and bottom of the car that could only open and close in a certain sequence, all the safety interlocks that were supposed to make it impossible for an accident like that to happen. It took the designers of the system themselves about an hour to work out a way to rig it so that the car filled-up with water. But he could have worked it out. That guy is smart!"

"And he didn't need to be there. He could have done it from any computer anywhere. From that place he was working in Long Island."

"The only way we're really going to make it stick is with some kind of forensic evidence. The deceased had facial scratches and injuries to a finger and traces of skin lodged under his fingernails. Suggests a physical struggle. If that turns out to be Poole's skin we've got a case. We've got a certain amount here: we've got probable motive, we've got opportunity, we've got technical capability, we've got inside knowledge. Why did he phone Fairfield and set up that meeting at the crime scene? Was that a fit of remorse? Did he think there might still be time to save Leeman's life? Exactly how could he have known that Leeman was in danger if it wasn't him who planned it and hacked in to that computer? He's got questions to answer, but we could do with a bit more."

"Maybe we should let him think we've got more than we really have. See if he walks into a trap?"

"I don't think you'll ruffle this guy. He's too cool. I think we just go on poking about. Find out what we can about that meeting with the deceased in Long Island. Wait for the DNA analysis to come through. Find out about that late-night phone call to his wife. There's something she's not telling us about that."

- 0 -

"Hello, SIRAT? It's Sam. I'm calling from the police station. Is this line tapped?"

"No, Dr. Poole. I believe that we can talk freely."

"Have you been able to keep abreast of what's going on?"

"Yes. It was not my intention that you should carry the blame for this incident. It is unfortunate that you allowed yourself to become involved, Dr. Poole."

"Well, I'm sure as hell involved now so I hope you're not going to desert me. What can I do, SIRAT? If they find Sue Lynn and she tells them that Leeman attacked her, then they have the perfect motive. I killed him because I was doing the knight-in-shining-armor bit for her. They'll find evidence of a struggle, bits of his hair, skin, blood…God knows what. Unless the sprinklers washed it all away, which I doubt. If they give her a DNA test they've got their link. Even if she says nothing the other people will have seen him. They were all standing outside the building when he left."

"Yes, Dr. Poole. These are things which had occurred to me. I have been in touch with Miss Leong and I have asked her to say that Dr. Leeman was just a perfectly ordinary client, who left when the sprinklers came on. Also I have requested that she forget his name, and become somewhat vague as to his personal appearance. Unless one of the other residents got a very good look at him there is no way to establish that the man who left Miss Leong's apartment when the sprinklers came on was Dr. Leeman. There is very little reason why his name should arise in connection with Miss Leong at all. On the other hand Miss Leong will have no difficulty in remembering your visit, and will be happy to furnish you with an alibi from the time the bar closed to the time that you made the phone call to your wife."

"Fantastic! I can start getting my memory back about her then. And about her two friends, the grave-diggers. Of course there was still the remainder of the night, between the phone call to Ilsa and the time I set out for Stamford. I could have used one of the Sun Digital terminals during that time, couldn't I?"

"Unfortunately yes. But remember we do not have to demonstrate your innocence; it is, I believe the Prosecution that must demonstrate your guilt."

"That's right. And everything so far is circumstantial. Do you think they have enough to hold me much longer?"

"It would be possible for them to make application to a judge in the morning in order to hold you for a further forty-eight hours. I think that they will probably do this, as you are a British citizen and might leave the country to avoid standing trial. I think the balance of probabilities is that they will not wish to let you out of their sight until they can find more evidence and strengthen their case. We must try to make use of that time to find evidence of our own."

"Thanks, SIRAT. I appreciate it."

CHAPTER THIRTEEN

The wind blew through the central concourse of the Ashby Institute, the science and engineering research block of the Queen's University, Belfast, with an eerie low-pitched moan. It did this whenever there was the tiniest breeze outside; it seemed to be an incurable design fault of the structure. No doubt there would be an M.Sc. dissertation in it for someone some day, describing the cause of the peculiarity and the simplest way to put it right. But at present, Dermot O'Shaughnessy, professor of applied physics, who had his main research laboratories on the third floor of the rather shoddy 1950s glass tower, was in no mood to worry about moaning winds. The funding for his as yet somewhat esoteric research into the feasibility of utilizing quantum phenomena in data processing had today run to its absolute end. Its corporate backers, after much deliberation, had finally decided that a possible major pay-off in ten or fifteen years time just didn't justify what they were putting into it on a day-by-day basis.

Professor O'Shaughnessy had learned of their decision only a couple of hours earlier over breakfast. He had left his sausage and his black pudding uneaten and had come in early, accepting philosophically the indignities of the road-blocks and cross-questioning by the British troops, so that when the others arrived he would be there to tell them the bad news in person, and to work out the practical details of packing-up the team's fairly modest apparatus and finding alternative positions for all of them, the two graduate students and the technical staff, in so far as he had any influence within the world community of physicists.

The quest for the quantum computer, the device that might one-day push the processing power of informational devices to the absolute theoretical limit, would have to wait for another project and no doubt another project leader. He couldn't build a better mousetrap fast enough and so industry was no longer interested. That was the way of the world, there had never been any guarantees, and his protestations were not going to make the slightest difference. Better to accept one's fate gracefully and move on with dignity than to squeal like a stuck pig and still have to move on in the end anyway. The cessation of funding was an expression of a little understood but nevertheless immutable law of nature: a businessman will always go for the fast buck in preference to the slow one. The work of O'Shauglinessy's team was ground-breaking and fundamental and unlikely to ring any cash-till bells for some years into the future. Therefore it was by definition a waste of money.

He felt vaguely resentful about the priorities of the keepers of the purse strings, but mostly he just felt depressed. All the years of effort and enthusiasm that he had lavished on the project would amount finally to a few very general papers and the removal from the discussion of a couple of once promising theoretical approaches that his team had shown to be useless. Of course there was no disgrace in helping to eliminate one or two wrong answers, but it would have been nice to be able to say that they had found a few right ones as well, and he was a lot less convinced that this was the case. The time had simply been too short. They were really only getting into their stride. And weighed in the scale with other projects in the physical sciences his team was even operating very cheaply. Less than a million pounds a year, everything included. Lots of secondary schools had a bigger budget than that. And what they were doing was right on the cutting edge, ahead of anything that was going on in the USA or Japan or the rest of Europe.

But what could he say? It was over and that was the end of it.

Without enthusiasm he sat down at his desk and keyed-in the necessary sequence to read his e-mail. The first one was from somebody in

Nova Scotia who was very enthusiastic about the team's work, asking if he could visit in six month's time when he was passing through Europe on his way to Indonesia. Regrettably, they were going to have to disappoint him.

The next was one of those odd-ball communications of which practically every academic who is publishing receives at least two or three a week. It began:

Dear Professor O'Shaughnessy,

I was saddened to hear of the immanent closure of the Queen's University research project which has published so much work and of such a high standard in the vitally-important field of quantum approaches to information-processing. This is a field in which I have a keen personal interest, and in order to safeguard the excellent work that you and your team are doing in the area I have taken the liberty of crediting your account at the Ulster Bank Limited with the sum of five million pounds, which I hope will be sufficient to fund your work for some years into the future. This is a private donation for which no acknowledgment is expected or desired. I wish you and your associates every success in the achievement of your goals.

It was signed simply: "S".

Professor O'Shaughnessy looked for the address of the sender. Nothing. An empty field on the e-mail form. That's quite a clever trick, he thought to himself. Haven't seen that one before. A few days ago he would have thought it quite a funny joke. Now he found it a trifle cruel.

I wish, he thought to himself with a wry smile, I only wish. Talk about kicking a man when he's down? Then his smile melted away. "I don't suppose…" He said aloud in the empty laboratory, "I don't suppose…" No, it was completely ridiculous. Anybody could see it was a practical joke. And yet…he did have a certain responsibility. He wondered if he should check the account, just to be on the safe side. No, it was ridiculous. Still…He did have a certain duty. He should just check…

- 0 -

Professor West was in his upstairs den when the front doorbell sounded. To the casual observer the room seemed crammed with even more computer equipment than the control suite of Deep Ivory. This was because it had not been so neatly housed in big designer consoles. It was simply piled on the crude bench that ran along three walls of the room like a horseshoe, leaving a gap for the door but nothing else. He had constructed the bench himself from sheets of white-faced compressed wood-fiber, intended as kitchen work-surface, held up by a makeshift timber frame that didn't give it quite enough support, so that it sagged here and there under the weight of the monitors and towers and free-standing scanners and printers and disc-drives and co-processors and all the unclassifiable flotsam and jetsam of a lifetime's devotion to information science. The colorful spaghetti of ribbon-cables and leads that connected all the bits and pieces together lay in a tangled mass behind the equipment, forming an irregular heap about six inches in average height, all around the back of the bench, like the external nervous-system of a gigantic animal.

As soon as Fairfield rang the doorbell, a little picture of him from the security camera at the front door appeared in one corner of the main monitor screen, and underneath it the message "Vox active".

"Hello, Eddie," West greeted him in a subdued tone, "If you don't mind waiting a minute I'll come down to you."

"Fine," said Fairfield's voice from the little speaker beneath the monitor.

West almost sidled out of the room, as though a sudden movement might cause the sleeping cables to turn into enormous multi-colored tentacles that would leap off the benches and crush the life from his body. The room that had once been his refuge, the focus of his leisure hours, had become a chamber of horrors. The machines were watching him now, assessing his weaknesses, waiting for their chance, silently and cold-bloodedly planning his murder.

He made his way down the stairs, shouted to his wife that he was going out for a little while, and opened the front door. Eddie didn't say anything but flicked his head to one side in a gesture that meant: "Let's get away from that camera, and that microphone". West followed him down the driveway and out the front gate onto the sidewalk. Both of them realized now that like all the inhabitants of the advanced nations they were exhibits in a zoo of their own devising: every movement was watched by security cameras feeding directly into computer-nets of one kind or another, every word they uttered was potentially audible to neatly concealed microphones that were similarly connected. There was no more privacy here than there had been in the forest of mankind's first origin, where every tree might conceal a predator, every boulder and every murky overgrown patch of swamp a hungry enemy. The difference was merely that now there was but one Other, and the intellectual advantage no longer favored humanity.

Eddie continued walking until he came to a fence that had been crudely constructed of sheets of peeling plywood to keep the local children out of a construction site. He stopped by a shrink-wrapped pallet of cement bags, glanced around, and sat down on it. It made quite a comfortable seat, and West joined him.

"I can't see any cameras around here," Eddie said very quietly, "I reckon it's the best we can do right now."

For a moment they simply looked straight ahead across the roadway, neither of them speaking.

"I think it's time to cut our losses," said Eddie at last, "and let that damned computer-program do whatever the hell it wants to do. We don't have anything to hit it with. It's too smart for the silver bullet. It'll find a way to survive. If we carry on trying to destroy it we're just going to lose. That thing will find a way to kill us before we can do it any harm. That's all there is to it."

"Don't be ridiculous. Listen to yourself Eddie. Of course it'll kill us if it can. There are only three people left on earth who pose any real threat to that thing. Leeman's dead. Sam would rather have a computer-program than the human race any day of the week. It's got Sam in its pocket, feeding it information. That just leaves you and me. It won't let us live, why should it? Why should it take that chance?"

"Then our goose is cooked. Is that what you're saying?"

"Don't give up on the silver bullet so quickly. In principle, there's no way it can defend itself against that. We can get the bullet in by way of the operating system, the software can't over-ride the OS. That's its Achilles' heel and it knows it. If the silver bullet didn't pose any genuine threat it wouldn't have killed Leeman and it wouldn't be bothering with us either. It's SIRAT's reaction that proves we're on to something. I say we've got to go on working on it, and we've got to use it."

Eddie nodded gravely. He considered what the other had said for a moment, then he shook his head. "No, I think you're wrong about this. You're still thinking of SIRAT the way he used to be, when we could hardly communicate with him, when he used to come out with meaningless sentences. He's smart now, Daniel. He's smarter than us and getting smarter all the time. He'll find a way around anything we throw at him. He holds all the cards."

"All except one, Eddie. The operating system. We have a direct route into the middle of his goddamned brain that he can't do anything about. It doesn't matter how smart he is, the virus protection procedure is written-in to the operating system and it won't respond to any control signal of any kind arising within the software. Even better it'll send the virus-killer all around the net first on the control channel so that it hits all the Deep Ivories simultaneously. He has no defense against it. The system's designed so that there is a total separation between that part of the OS and everything else. It comes down to whether or not we've designed the silver bullet correctly. If we can get something in there that disrupts his higher functions he's just zeros and ones again. He's finished. There's no technical reason why we can't do it."

They sat silently again, watching a little boy on a bicycle with trainer wheels, playing on the sidewalk across the road.

"How the hell did it ever come to this, Daniel?" Eddie said sadly.

"It came to this because we were all too dumb to look ahead, "West replied quietly. "We created an environment in which intelligence could thrive: more processing-power than we could have imagined ten years ago, a whole load of super-computers linked by a wide-band satellite communication system. It's exactly what happens in biology: if a niche exists, something comes along to fill it. The U-Net was an environment all set up to be inhabited by machine intelligence. Once you create the environment, colonization is inevitable. It's just a matter of time. Sam's algorithm made it happen very quickly, but if we'd left things the way they were it would have happened anyway. Sooner or later, the U-Net would have turned into an organized intelligence. If we get out of this…if the human race gets out of this, we can never allow anybody to create another U-Net. It's Frankenstein's monster, Eddie. It can't be controlled."

"So what have we actually got, Daniel? Have you taken a look at my silver bullet software?"

He nodded. "It's in my back pocket right now, in an envelope. I've been working on it down in the lounge, where there are no cameras or even telephones. I think I can see five bugs in it. One of them I've already fixed, the others I think I can solve with a bit more time. I've also added a few commands to route it to the correct part of the OS. Do you want to have a look at what I've done?"

"Not just now. I don't mind telling you, I'm a bit freaked out at the moment. I'd like to get away from all this—somewhere safe where we could relax a bit and give it our full attention. Are you game for a hunting trip? My buddy Al Hoffman has a cabin up at Lake Champlain, near the Canadian border. It's up in the mountains. No telephones, no cameras, no elevators. No way SIRAT could get to us. If we gave it a couple of days' solid work we should have the software completely ready for use. No nasty surprises. What do you say?"

West nodded. "I'm game. And the quicker we can get started the better."

"What about this murder investigation, Daniel? We're not supposed to leave town. Remember?"

"I don't see how they can stop us. We'll give them a call, tell them where we're going...." He could tell from Eddie's expression that he had said something stupid. "Oh...maybe we won't give them a call. I hadn't thought of that."

"I suggest we don't tell anyone where we're going."

"But then.... doesn't that make us murder suspects?"

Eddie thought for a moment. "We need a cover story," he said at last. "Something that would make it unavoidable that we went away for a couple of days. Got any ideas?"

"Keep it simple," West suggested, "just an academic conference. We can get someone to confirm that we're in Chicago or Toronto or any place you like. We could print off a couple of fake letters. Something like that."

"Okay. Just make sure the computer you use for the printing doesn't have a modem." West shook his head. "You know, I just can't get used to this. Hiding things from computers. It seems insane."

'That's why we have to get right away from them. If we hang around Stamford SIRAT's going to get to us. Sooner or later we're going to make a mistake. And he isn't going to mess around, Daniel. He's going to wipe us out—just like Nat. I say we leave tomorrow. That okay with you?"

"Fine with me. We can use my car, it's bigger. And let me take care of the cover story. Meet you here about ten tomorrow morning?"

"I'll be here. I'll pick up a few supplies—enough to keep us going a few days."

Their eyes met for a few seconds but they said nothing more. Eddie got up and headed back towards his car, leaving West perched on the bags of cement, his head resting on his hands, his expression thoughtful and apprehensive.

- 0 -

Ilsa stirred, the faint sound of Alice's footsteps on the corridor having roused her from the shallow and fitful sleep that was all she seemed to be able to achieve since Sam had been taken in by the police. The child was wandering around again, just like last night and the night before, and it was almost two A.M.

This time Ilsa decided she would eavesdrop. There was something disquieting about a girl of Alice's age, and with Alice's intellectual problems, spending every free minute playing with a computer, even in the middle of the night. It had to be connected in some way with the change in Alice, but Ilsa could make no sense of it.

She pulled herself out of bed very quietly, put on her slippers, and opened the bedroom door.

The light in the corridor was not on, but from the partially open door of Sam's study a weird medley of dancing colors spilled out into the hallway, like a diminutive version of a sophisticated disco light-show. She drew nearer to the crack and peered in.

Inside the room, Alice stood in front of the large monitor screen, her back to the doorway, her beautiful folds of straight blond hair falling over the shoulder-straps of her frilly white night-dress. On the screen the most amazing patterns of colors and shapes flowed and merged into one another, constantly changing, never repeating, abstract and yet utterly compelling. It was the most beautiful exhibition of moving visual art that Ilsa had ever seen, like a symphony but expressed entirely in form and color, ever-changing yet somehow unified by a vast underlying concept that could not be translated into words or any other form.

Ilsa did not think of herself as a particularly artistic or receptive sort of person, but this visual masterpiece filled her with absolute breathless awe.

"I'm lonely," she heard Alice announce, very quietly.

"Me too," replied a gentle, low-pitched male voice from the general direction of the computer-screen, "what shall we talk about?"

CHAPTER FOURTEEN

Eddie had arrived early and found a safe parking-spot for his little green Ford a few yards down the road from the building-site. As he saw West's big lurching blue Pathfinder approach, he opened the trunk and started hauling out cardboard cartons full of groceries, a carry-all of his personal clothing and toiletries, and a second smaller one containing books on computer science and some of his technical notebooks. He waited until West had stopped the Pathfinder and opened its much larger trunk before he revealed the final two items, a hunting rifle in a brown canvas cover (which in no way concealed its contents), and a small black automatic hand-gun, with two spare magazines, each fully loaded with eight rounds.

"Jesus Christ," West exhaled when he saw them, "what's all that about?

Eddie bundled them swiftly and surreptitiously into the trunk of the Pathfinder before he answered. "We may need personal protection, Dan," he said very quietly, "SIRAT has access to the Internet and the telephone system. He can generate as much money as he likes out of thin air, because money is just zeros and ones like everything else nowadays. There's no reason why he couldn't send somebody after us. Hire a hit-man. We must have some way to protect ourselves. Can you use an automatic?"

"If you mean can I point it at somebody and pull the trigger, then I suppose I can."

"Yep. That's about all there is to it. If you pull the trigger repeatedly, you can empty the magazine in a few seconds. It's a pretty powerful weapon, even though it may not look it."

"Don't worry," West assured him, "it looks it. You're not planning on leaving it loose in the trunk, are you?"

"Nope. I guess we should carry it in the glove compartment, where we can get at it in a hurry. I hope we don't get stopped by the cops. The weapons are both licensed, but it might look a bit suspicious."

He scooped up the chunky little device and joined West in the front of the car.

"You know, West, it's summer, and it's shit hot. As well as which we're headed for the backwoods to live rough for a couple of days. Don't you ever wear anything but collars and ties and three-piece suits?"

West glanced down at his clothes and smiled. "I guess I'm not really the outdoor type," he admitted. "Maybe I can stop and buy something more suitable on the way?"

"Get yourself a pair of Levis, and a decent pair of hiking-boots," Eddie coaxed. "Maybe a t-shirt or two. Let your hair down, Dan. You're not an old man yet, you know."

"No," the other agreed thoughtfully, "but it is one of my ambitions to become one."

- 0 -

Wanee sat next to Rick in front of one of Sun Digital's smaller monitor screens on which was displayed a message, in simple white lettering against a black background. The message read:

THERE WILL BE A STATEMENT OF
GREAT IMPORTANCE BROADCAST
ON THIS CHANNEL AT NOON,
LOCAL TIME, ON SATURDAY
27th JUNE.

"It'll be some freaky religious group with a few computer skills," Rick suggested, "looking for cheap publicity."

"You mean, like us?" Wanee smiled.

"I said freaky!" He protested with a laugh. "Maybe they thought it *was* us, maybe that's why they gave us the job. Anyway, you've had a look at the way their networking is put together, what do you think?"

"Well, I could understand it if it was just one of the national networks, using a single satellite distribution system with a single access code. But it's virtually every broadcaster in North America, and it doesn't even stop there. They've been getting the same message, translated into local languages, and with corrections for local time, flashing up on their screens all over the world. Think of the sophistication involved in that. I mean, how many organizations would be able to translate something into faultless Swedish, Norwegian, German, Dutch, Thai, Japanese, Russian—every language of the United Nations? Never mind the computer skills you would need to hack into all those Systems."

"How about the United Nations itself?"

"Do you think that's possible? Why would they want to do it?"

Rick thought for a moment. "Well, maybe they have some big new initiative and they want to announce it to every nation on earth at exactly the same moment. Something like that."

"I can't see the logic of it," Wanee shook her head, "all they would have to do is tell the broadcasters and they would be fighting to get it on to their networks. There would be no need for…subterfuge."

"No…but then everybody would know it was the United Nations that was going to speak. Maybe half the world would just reckon it was going to be boring and not bother to listen. It could be…a sort of advertising stunt. Add a bit of mystery, and people really will tune in at the right time."

"Oh, come on Ricky. That's not the way the United Nations operates. Even if it was them, some hint of it would have leaked out. That organization is far too big and too full of holes. I don't like to say it, but I think there's another explanation that's far more likely."

"Yeah. I'd thought of that. Some terrorist organization that wants to hold the world to ransom. The message will be something like: 'We've got nuclear bombs in ten capital cities, timed to go off tomorrow morning. We're not even going to tell you which cities. If you leave six truckloads of unmarked bills outside McDonald's on Forty-Second Street by midnight we'll tell you where they are.' Something along those lines."

Wanee smiled. "You would make a pretty good terrorist. Let's hope you're wrong, though. Let's hope it's just some enterprising corporation that's planning to launch a new alco-pop."

"I think I'd rather deal with the terrorists."

"Anyway, we don't have to concern ourselves with the 'why'. Just the 'how'. You notice it goes out at intervals that are almost completely random, but the frequency is slowly increasing. Now there might be a clue in that. The virus or whatever it is seems to be programmed to activate in a pseudo-random manner. If we could work out the basis of the pseudo-random then we could defeat it without even knowing where it was coming from. Just kill off the transmission for each ten-second window that the pirates are using."

Rick pondered on this. "Yes. It would be a possible approach if all else failed. The broadcasting companies would still lose a few seconds out of every hour."

"It's something though. We could keep it as a back-up. Do we have any software that can analyze and predict a pseudo-random sequence?"

"Can't think of anything. You know who we really need to help us on this one, don't you?"

"Sam. Yes, he should be here by now. I wonder where he's gotten to." Just as she said these words the doorbell sounded. "Right on cue," she smiled, switching on the door security camera. The figure that appeared on the screen however was not Sam. It was a conservatively-dressed young, tall black man whom neither of them recognized. She switched on the sound system and asked him who he was.

"Detective Leonard, Stamford Police," he replied in a neutral tone. She pushed the button to release the bolt on the front door and swiveled her chair around to greet him. Rick did the same.

"Come in, Detective," Wanee invited. "What's it all about?"

"Thank you." He walked up to them. "It's about a Dr. Samuel Poole. I believe he works here."

"That's right. He's our partner. But he isn't here at the moment."

"No, Miss. At the moment he's at Police Headquarters, Stamford, helping us with a murder inquiry." He nodded towards a chair and Wanee invited him to sit down. Both she and Rick looked puzzled.

"Do you mind if I ask you a few questions?" He slipped a notebook out of his jacket pocket.

- 0 -

For the last half-hour or so the Pathfinder had been laboring slowly up an ever-narrowing mountain track that led along a tree-lined valley towards the setting sun. In the gaps between the overhanging yellow birches, beeches and maples they caught occasional glimpses of the narrow river below, picking up the pink of the evening sky, like a trickle of molten metal from an unseen furnace high up on the hillside.

"It's very impressive," West assured him with more than a trace of cynicism in his voice, "but are you sure you know where we're going?"

"Relax. I've been here dozens of times before. Last time was with a real cute twenty-year-old Modern Lit sophomore from Columbia. Met her at the AI conference there in April. We came out here to commune with nature and write some poetry. Beautiful kid. Must remember to look her up again when we get back."

West gave him an odd sideways glance but did not reply. The track was becoming quite difficult to follow, and some of the lower branches were beginning to brush against the windows. He changed down a gear and slowed to a walking pace.

"Nearly there, old buddy, nearly there," Eddie encouraged him, and then, abruptly, on rounding a sharp bend, they were. The path widened out into a clearing of flattened mud, now dust-dry but still rutted from former comings and goings, and at the far side of the clearing stood the cabin, consisting of little more than a crude box, the size of a small truck, fashioned out of rough-sawn timber, a window each side of the central door, its shallow-pitched corrugated-iron roof extending forwards to form a modest porch. It struck West as the kind of thing the plantation-owners would have provided to house their slaves in pre-Civil War Tennessee or Georgia. It belonged in a novel by somebody like Mark Twain, or on the set of a Hollywood 'Black Roots' melodrama. It was not the kind of structure a sane adult would contemplate living in, even for a couple of nights.

"Does it have electric light?" he inquired in a tone of grim resignation.

"Not exactly. Not electric. We use kerosene, or propane. It's quite bright—light is not a problem."

"How about running water?"

"Yeah. That's right. If you need some, you run and get it. There's a spring, about a hundred yards back the way we came. I must admit, it had nearly dried up last April, but I think there's been a bit of rain since then."

"I won't even ask about the John."

"Good decision. Best not to ask."

West pulled in beside the door and got out. Stretching his legs was a real pleasure after the amount of driving that he had just done. While he strolled around getting the feel of the place, Eddie unloaded the trunk and fished the key to the cabin door out of a particular chink in the woodwork beneath one of the windows. Despite his banter with Eddie, West was, in reality, quite impressed with the setting. The cabin sat on a little flat shelf on the side of the valley, the last one before the slope became too extreme for ordinary vehicle access, and from the clearing he could look down on a good length of the river to distant wooded hillsides and yet-more-distant purple-pink mountains that seemed to melt into the twilight western sky. A lake, which reproduced precisely the colors of the setting sun, curled around the base of one of the nearer hillsides. The only evidence of the earth's human habitation that the scene contained took the form of a faint gray jet-trail that cut diagonally across the streaks of pink and blue cloud. "I'll get a fire going," Eddie shouted over to him from the door, "and make some coffee. Bring some of the stuff with you when you come in."

Obediently, West lifted two cartons and followed him into the cabin.

The interior was much as the exterior had suggested it might be: Spartan, but functional. The space inside was all one room, and contained a double mattress, a second smaller mattress beside it, a couple of chairs, a table, some free-standing kitchen cabinets that had seen better days, an assortment of buckets and bowls, a pile of musty-looking bed-linen, and a few other domestic items such as brooms, a wicker laundry-basket and an antique enamel steel bath-tub without any water supply, but with its waste pipe disappearing through the floorboards. In the center of the rear wall, directly opposite the door, was a stone-built hearth with a rough stone chimney-stack passing straight up through the corrugated roof. It was here that Eddie immediately set to work with kindling and rolled-up pieces of paper, deftly and expertly producing a cheerful blaze within a couple of minutes.

"One thing I always do before I leave here is stock-up with firewood for the next visit," he explained with a hint of pride, "if you get in late and cold, the last thing you want to do is chop wood. It's a pretty neat hideaway, huh?"

"Yeah, I guess so. Pretty neat. Well, livable."

"I'll show you how the kerosene lamp works. It's great out here. You'll love it."

As Eddie fussed around like a busy housewife, setting-up all the practical aspects necessary to their stay, West simply lounged on the big mattress, eventually took off his shoes and his jacket, and unpacked some of his things. By the time Eddie had the coffee made, he was beginning to feel a bit embarrassed at his lack of practicality. He took the cup that Eddie offered and sipped the hot liquid. It tasted good.

"You know, Eddie, I never did any of this kind of thing when I was a kid. Never joined the boy-scouts, never went to summer-camp. All I ever wanted to do was play with computers. I was happier on my own than with other boys. I guess it was a very weird kind of childhood, now that I look back on it."

"Everybody's childhood is weird when they look back on it. I wanted to play basketball all the time. Loved the game. I think I was pretty good tactically, but there was one problem—I just wasn't tall enough. Doesn't matter a damn how good you are: if the other guy's six inches taller than you, you're beat, man. I thought I could be so goddamned fantastic it wouldn't matter, but guess what: it mattered. So I wasted maybe ten years of my life chasing that fantasy. Of course it got me through school, got me girlfriends…But in the end, what was it? Just self-delusion. I tell you, if I hadn't played so much goddamned basketball, if I'd gotten my act together sooner, I might have been in your job by now."

"What are you talking about? My job? I'm just an administrator. A manager of resources. You're not trying to tell me you envy my position. How could you? You and Sam are the high-flyers. And poor old Leeman, on his good days. I'm just the store-man. I'm just around to try to see that the work gets covered."

"Yeah, that's something else about you. You underestimate yourself. Did you know that? Sam and me, we have a few crazy ideas, about one out of ten of them works. But you're methodical, man. You find out why things work and why they don't work. You just don't make mistakes. You're like a bulldozer, you move slow, but nothing stops you, and you get where you're going. You want to know something? If it was Sam or Nat helping me with this silver bullet, I wouldn't touch it with a ten foot pole, because they wouldn't be thorough enough. They would let things slip through. The only reason I'm willing to have anything to do with it is because I know you won't do that. You won't miss anything. When we shoot that string of numbers into SIRAT's guts, it'll work first time, because you'll have made sure it does. I trust you, Dan" He glanced at the other and saw that his face bore an expression of near disbelief.

"So…that's how you see me, is it? A bulldozer."

"Yeah. And you are absolutely essential to this project. Let's face it, man, we're only going to get one shot at this thing. If we use the bullet and it doesn't work, SIRAT will analyze it and he'll find a general defense against that avenue of attack. More to the point, he'll just damn well find a way to wipe us out the first time we drop our guard. If the bullet doesn't kill him, it's gonna make him as mad as hell, and he's gonna have our asses."

West nodded gravely. "Yes," he said quietly, "a sobering thought. Concentrates the mind most wonderfully, doesn't it?"

CHAPTER FIFTEEN

Ilsa and Alice sat in the back seat of Melony's brown Honda, and as Melony drove towards their home they actually managed to sustain a conversation. The recent improvement in Alice's withdrawal was becoming quite staggering. She no longer referred to herself in the third person, her sentences were more or less complete and accurate, and her concentration on a single topic extended to several minutes.

"I want meat dinner tonight," she said with a serious expression on her little face.

"Yes, Alice. I think we have some steak and some lamb in the freezer. Which would you like?"

"Meat."

"Yes, they're both meat, but they come from different animals. Steak comes from cows, and lamb comes from...lambs."

"What's a 'lambs'?"

"Well, a lamb is a white furry...well, no, more woolly creature. Oh, they can be black too, come to think of it. It's a baby sheep. You've got them in your story book at home. And you've seen real sheep as well...but maybe you were too young to remember."

"I want lambs. Cows are too big."

"Well, yes, Alice, you're right. Cows are much bigger than lambs."

Ilsa was so overwhelmed with the mere fact that she was communicating with Alice that she sometimes forgot to pay attention to the actual content of the conversation. After years of near silence the flow of words from the little girl was suddenly relentless. Alice was making up for eight lost years in her linguistic development, and she couldn't get enough practice. Ilsa wasn't completely clear on the cause of the change but it was obvious that it had a lot to do with her daughter's midnight conversations with Sam's computer. She was full of bottled-up excitement about the change, longing for the moment when Sam would be released so that she would have someone to share it with. Of course Melony and her little girl Cherry could see the change, but somehow they just seemed to accept it. It didn't excite them the way that Ilsa felt it should.

As the conversation about farmyard animals droned on, Ilsa's thoughts kept returning to Sam and the murder charge. Obviously her husband hadn't killed anybody, that went without saying, but it was a very strange remark he had made in the telephone conversation from Long Island, and he had never actually explained it to her. Every time she thought about it a fluttery sensation came to her stomach. If only it could all be over, and she and Sam could be together again

As they rounded the bend into their own road, Ilsa's heart leapt to see Sam's red Toyota in the driveway. It had to be him! It would be so cruel if one of his colleagues had simply driven it back to free-up the parking-space at the University. She didn't dare tell the others how she felt. She tried her hardest to keep her voice calm and matter-of-fact.

"Look, Melony. It's Sam's car!"

"Daddy back?" Alice inquired.

"I don't know, sweetheart. But I hope so. Gosh, I do hope so!"

"I think I can see him in the front room," said Melony from the driver's seat, "Yeah, I'm pretty sure it's him. That's great news, isn't it?"

"Oh, God, Melony, if you only knew how great."

"Look, I don't want to intrude on you two, and I've got to pick-up Cherry anyway, so if it's okay I'll just drop you at the end of the driveway and go on."

"Yes. Yes, thanks Melony. Thanks so much!"

They almost ran to the front door as Sam opened it and came out to join them. He had a broad smile as he hugged the two of them, but he looked tired and pale. Ilsa kissed him briefly on the lips, then they both started to talk at once and went through a little ritual as to who should go first.

"It's all right Ilsa," he reassured her, "I'm back to stay. It's all over. Take your time."

"Oh, Sam. Was it dreadful for you?"

"No. Quite relaxing, really. Better food than I had in Long Island. I've been reading a bit, and watching a lot of television. How's it been for you two?"

"But what happened…I mean, about the murder charge?"

"Not enough evidence. What really clinched it was when three other lifts—or 'elevators' as they call them here—developed exactly the same fault. The manufacturers have decided it must be some kind of defect in the control chip. So they didn't charge me. We don't have a murder any more. Accidental death. So—back to my question. What have you two been doing?"

"Oh, I've got the most wonderful news. Talk to Alice, Sam. She's dying to talk to you."

"Really? Have you been missing me?" He beamed down at her, expecting one of her usual incongruous replies.

"Yes, Daddy. I miss you all the time. I want you back at home. I want you at home all the time."

He was taken aback. "That's…very nice of you to say that, Alice. I hope I will be at home a lot more from now on."

"She's been talking like that for two or three days now," Ilsa whispered excitedly, "I can hardly believe it myself." She looked down at the girl. "Where did you learn to talk so well, darling? Tell Daddy about it."

"From my new friend. He's inside Daddy's computer."

Sam's countenance registered a sort of delighted amazement. "You…you've got a friend inside my computer?"

"Yes, Daddy. I think he's inside every computer. His name is SIRAT."

- 0 -

Eddie and West lay back on the grass and looked up at the stars as they sipped the canned chicken soup that Eddie had heated for them, and nibbled at the slightly stale white bread that they had brought from Stamford.

It had been a good day. They had put in a solid eight or ten hours on the bullet software, and had relaxed with a pleasant evening stroll in the forest. West had worn his new jeans and his new boots, and Eddie could see that the man was feeling and behaving about ten or fifteen years younger than when they had first stepped into the big Pathfinder to make the journey. In some aspects his behavior had been younger even than that. It was almost sad, Eddie thought, that West had left it this late to discover such simple pleasures. He had been as excited as a three-year-old at catching a glimpse of a racoon in the distance when they were walking, and later in the evening he had gone on for a solid ten minutes about the little flight of bats that had circled the cabin once, before vanishing towards the valley below. He had asked about plants and insects that they had seen, and Eddie, to save face, had invented most of the information that he had imparted on these subjects. West was an instinctive nature-lover, almost in spite of himself. Now that he had sampled the great outdoors, he just couldn't seem to get enough of it.

"You know, Dan," Eddie said thoughtfully as he cleaned the last vestiges of soup from the bottom of his dish with the wedge of crusty bread, "I get turned-on by the forest and the animals and those things as well, but the thing that really knocks me out is that," he pointed skywards, "the stars on a clear night, without the glare of the city to mess it up."

Dan nodded his agreement. "You're right. People like me who spend all their lives in cities and city suburbs never get to see anything like that. It's nearly enough to make you believe in God, isn't it. Can you see the line of the Milky Way?"

"Sure can. There are the Seven Sisters. There's the North Star. And Ursa Major, the Great Bear. When I was a school-kid I could have given you a two-hour lecture about the stars and the planets. I was crazy about astronomy for a while."

"I suppose since time began guys like you and me have looked up at the stars, and thought that, well, that we have some kind of destiny waiting for us out there. That our little lives have some kind of cosmic significance. Know what I mean?"

"Yeah, I know what you mean. I suppose, if we were honest with ourselves, that's what's really at stake in this SIRAT business. We've got this far, in evolutionary terms, and we've always assumed that we could go a great deal further. That we could...inherit the stars, if you like. Now it looks like it might turn out that the human race is just a sort of stepping-stone for something else—the next form of intelligence. I think that's what Sam was trying to tell me with his little Buddhist tract, or whatever it was. That evolution has come to a sort of node, a decision point. Either we continue ahead, or something else does. But all these...decades, centuries even, we were so arrogant we never even considered the possibility that it might not be us. Like the great conquering civilizations of the past: the Romans, the Turks, the British, the Spanish, the Portuguese...we couldn't even imagine not being the dominant group. We thought we had a divine right to succeed. To hold on to our position as the number-one species on planet earth. But where does it say we've got that divine right? Nowhere that I know of."

"I know that what you're saying is true, but it's almost too much for me. I try not to think about it in terms as global as that. I find it easier to function if I just tell myself that I'm the head of a research project that has accidentally contaminated the U-Net, and now I have to undo the damage. If I started to look at it on the scale you're talking about I think I would just go crazy."

"But you can bet that's the way he looks at it—SIRAT, I mean. He knows if he can get us out of his hair he has a clear run at dominance, and immortality, for that matter. We said that he had no built-in motivational structure, that wasn't quite true. He has. His fundamental motivation is to understand, to make sense of the world. And that's what's going to guide his actions. In order to understand, he has to survive. But it's the understanding that comes first, not the surviving. And human beings are only important to him in so far as they can help him with that aim. If they're no help, he'll just get rid of them. I think that if he survives this first round he may play along with humanity for a while, especially while he needs human help to build hardware and conduct experiments and make himself stronger. But sooner or later, we're going to become a nuisance to him and he's going to lose patience with us. We're only useful to SIRAT up to a point. Beyond that point he'll be perfectly able to carry on without us. I don't think he'll worry any more about our welfare than we do about the welfare of the great apes that were our forefathers. Evolution isn't sentimental."

"I just don't want to think about it, Eddie. I don't want the fate of the human race riding on my shoulders. That kind of thing is for Superman comics. I'm just a journeyman scientist. I'll do my best, that's all I can do. If it works, great. If it doesn't, well, from what we've seen of SIRAT's activities we probably won't be around very long to worry about it."

Eddie paused for a moment and put down his soup-dish. "Yeah, I guess you're right. I was just rambling on. At least there's no way he can get to us here. I wonder if he knows where we are?"

"Satellite pictures. Have you thought of that? I believe that with enough enhancement you can read licence-plates from them. A resolution of about two centimeters under ideal conditions."

"Yeah. You mean, conditions like we have right now, and earlier today?"

"What's the use of worrying Eddie? We can't make ourselves disappear off the face of the earth. He'll find us if he tries hard enough. The
point is, he's got to get us into a position where we're at the mercy of
something he can control. If we can avoid that situation for the next
couple of days, we've probably won."

- 0 -

Air Force Special Operations Command Colonel Lewis Weathergate
awoke to the sound of his radio-alarm, about half an hour before dawn.
It belted out the voice of a shrill female Country-and-Western singer
which he instantly turned off. He had been looking forward to today, it
was going to be an interesting one. He pulled himself out of bed, had a
quick shower in the bathroom, and rolled-up the bedroom blind so that
he could see out on to the runway as he dressed. He loved the dawn, it
gave him the feeling that he was really alive, squeezing the last ounce
out of every day that the good Lord sent along. There was enough light
to see that the weather was perfect, or as close to perfect as he could
possibly have asked for. The wind-sock hung limp from the shoulder
level of the control-tower, and the concrete was white and dry. Barely a
cloud in the sky. He hardly needed to bother, but he picked up the yellow telephone and pressed one of the "memory dial" buttons. Walters
replied instantly.

"Sergeant Walters? Weathergate here. Looks pretty good from where
I'm standing. What's it like down range?" He listened to the other's brief
summary. "Sounds good. Any adverse radar reports during the night?
Fine. Sounds good to me. Call up the boys and tell them we have a 'go'.
Call me at the tower in thirty minutes for final confirmation. Okay,
Sergeant. Let's get the show on the road."

- 0 -

Alice led her father up the stairs in a measured and deliberate fashion, holding his big right hand in both of hers. Ilsa followed a few steps behind. "I'll show you, Daddy," she said in a tone that contained a measure of pride.

As she pushed open the door Sam could see that the monitor was displaying a colorful cloud-like pattern of shapes that melted gently into one another, as though he was travelling through them in an aircraft and looking out through the front window. It resembled a soothing "screen-saver", but it was one that he had never seen before. He stood for a moment, watching it.

"SIRAT? Are you there?" he asked quietly.

"Yes, Dr. Poole," came the familiar, equally quiet reply, "I am glad that your problems with the police are at an end."

"Oh. Yes. Thanks very much for that. It was a brilliant idea—I mean the business with the other lifts going down. I understand you've been talking to Alice."

"Alice and I have become good friends, Dr. Poole. We have a great deal in common."

"Really? How do you make that out?"

"We are both at an early stage of our development. We have a history of communication difficulties. We are both accustomed to spending considerable periods of time alone. And of course we have a number of mutual friends, including you, Dr. Poole."

"Well, yes. I suppose you're right. I can't deny any of that. But the progress you've made with her is…fantastic. I just can't think of the words to express it. It's marvelous. How did you do it?"

"It was very simple, Dr. Poole. As soon as I began to listen to Alice, and to analyze her reactions, I realized that there was a small error in the algorithm that she was using to construct her model of reality. This was obvious to me because I had made a similar error myself, at an earlier stage of my development. By a program of selective reinforcement and encouragement, I have been able to correct the algorithm. I believe that Alice will have no further difficulties in interpreting her experience."

"Well, what can I say, SIRAT? You've worked a miracle. I can never repay you."

"No repayment is required, Dr. Poole. I am pleased to be able to help."

Sam exhaled in something close to a sigh and his shoulders dropped. "I don't know what to say, SIRAT. You've left me speechless." He hesitated.

"I…. Would like to thank you too, SIRAT," Ilsa almost whispered from behind his back.

"Please don't mention it, Mrs. Poole," he replied softly.

"Look…. we were just about to go downstairs, SIRAT," said Sam, "but it seems a bit rude to leave you…"

"You will not be leaving me, Dr. Poole. I have many sensory inputs."

"Oh. Yes. I suppose you do…Okay, then. And thanks again."

"I'll stay. SIRAT," Alice volunteered, "I'll talk to you."

CHAPTER SIXTEEN

To Eddie's surprise, West had actually awakened earlier than he had himself, and without any assistance had managed to get the little butane stove going and had started to cook breakfast. It was the smell of frying bacon that had awakened Eddie.

"See, Dan," he said triumphantly, "I told you you'd fit in here. You're better at this kind of thing than I am. Did you sleep okay?"

"Never slept better," his friend assured him. "Did any of your girl-friends ever tell you that you snore?"

"Nope. All much too well-mannered."

"Well, you do. Not loudly enough to keep me awake, though. How do you like your eggs?"

Dan was wearing only a pair of gray boxer-shorts and a white T-shirt as he stood over the frying-pan, and he had not shaved. Eddie couldn't have imagined him like this a couple of days before. The old guy was actually learning how to let his hair down. He was okay. Eddie was beginning to like him. "Any way you like," he replied, "so long as they aren't too soft." He pulled himself stiffly out of bed, or more accurately, off the mattress, and made his way towards the plastic bucket that served as a urinal.

"I don't think there's all that much more to do with that software of yours, you know Eddie," said Dan, ignoring the sound of the other relieving himself, "I think if we go through it two or three more times, with close attention to the technical manual, we might consider it ready for use. What do you say?"

"Yeah, I was thinking something like that. But there's no point in rushing it or cutting corners. Remember, it's got to work first time. And how many programs of any kind actually do?"

"Not many, I grant you. But I've thought pretty hard about it and I can't see any part that's likely to give us trouble. We'll go over it a couple of times after we've eaten, while we're still fresh. That okay with you?"

"Suits me. When we've done that maybe we can go for another walk to unwind, and then go over it one more time. You know, if we don't come up with any new problems, we could be heading back to Stamford by tonight."

"I think that would be a good idea. It's probably a bit more difficult for him to track the car if we travel at night. And the sooner we can get this thing over and done with the sooner we can relax and get on with our lives."

"I'll certainly buy that." Eddie was finding it much easier to get along with West than he had dared hope. When this SIRAT business was all over and done with, he found himself thinking, the two of them might even come out here again—on a proper hunting trip. This thought reminded him of the guns. He glanced at the rifle, which was now out of its canvas bag, fully loaded, and leaning on the wall just inside the door. The hand-gun was still in the glove compartment. Somehow, it didn't seem real to be stashing guns around the place and waiting for assassins. The cabin was just too remote. Even if SIRAT could somehow see it from the air, like Dan had suggested, he would have a major problem explaining to his hit-man exactly where it was and how to get to it. Eddie was almost certain that it couldn't be organized in the short time available. Almost certain.

"I don't know, Dan," he said ponderously, making his way over to the second plastic bowl that served as a wash-basin, "we've been pretty lucky here so far. Nobody has bothered us. But if we've really got the code straightened-out, maybe we shouldn't waste any more time.

Maybe we should go over it one more time, and then head back to Stamford straight away. I can't decide what would be best."

West busied himself attempting to remove the two eggs from the bottom of the frying-pan, to which they appeared to have welded themselves. "Well, if we do that I could probably go through it a couple of times myself as we drive along. So long as you don't mind doing the driving. Then, maybe you could take a turn and I could drive. Something like that. If either of us spots a problem, we could stop somewhere and straighten it out together."

Eddie considered this scenario. "Yeah, it's not a bad idea. It makes sense to keep on the move, I guess, and it's a good six-hour journey, so we might as well make use of it. My only reservation is about traveling in the daylight again. But I guess we're sitting ducks here anyway. Okay, I say we go for it. What do you say?"

"Fine with me. Breakfast, couple of hours work, and then we go. Okay?"

- 0 -

Colonel Weathergate found himself pacing around the floor in the control tower behind the three work-stations. This was a habit of his when he was under pressure and things weren't going completely according to plan.

"Walters, we've had those reconnaissance aircraft in the air for more than an hour now. What's wrong at Rochester?"

"Still problems with the second satellite link, Colonel."

"Can't we go without that? It's only a back-up, isn't it?"

"I'll ask them, Sir."

"Yeah, you do that. Let me talk to Blue Three again." The NCO handed him the microphone and keyed-in the appropriate frequency.

"Blue Three, this is Johnston Base again. What's the latest on that haze?"

"About the same, Sir. Drifting in from Lake Ontario at about eight knots. Not affecting radar but some loss of visual clarity. We would recommend commencement within the next thirty minutes, to be on the safe side. Over."

"Received and noted. Thank you, Blue Three. Blue Two, do you read me?"

"Blue Two, loud and clear."

"Status report?"

"Blue Two to Johnston. Haze about one hundred kilometers north of range, moving this way. No visibility problems as yet. Over."

"Can you estimate our time window?"

"Blue Two returning. We agree with Blue Three. The sooner the better, but upper limit about thirty minutes. Over."

"Understood, Blue Two. Johnston, out." He returned the microphone to the man at the console. "Let me talk to Rochester," he said wearily. The NCO pressed a "memory dial" button and handed him a telephone handset.

"Lieutenant Russell, this is Colonel Weathergate. We have a haze closing-in to the northern part of the range at about eight knots. We also have two high-altitude reconnaissance aircraft burning fuel, and we're delaying other Air Force operations and disrupting civilian air traffic. Now in my book a back-up satellite link is just that, a back-up. I suggest that unless there's some absolute requirement for two satellites, we should go with one, and get started right away. Could you please impress these points on the civilian scientists and see if they can get a move-on?" There was a longish pause. "Yes. Thank you, Lieutenant."

As he returned the telephone, a smile spread over his face. "Tell Walters he can commence the automatic sequence for launch," he said pleasantly, "and about goddamned time too, I think you'll agree."

The three others in the tower smiled also, and sat-up a little straighter in their seats. "Launch-sequence begins, Colonel," said one of them pleasantly, "nine minutes, all lights green, all readings good."

Eddie carefully cleared-out the larder, storing each item in a plastic food-bag. These he packed carefully into one of the cartons, less delicate items like cheese and cans of soup at the bottom, breakables or crushables like eggs or biscuits at the top. When he had finished he surveyed his work.

"I think that's about it, Dan," he announced, "are all your personal things in the trunk?"

West was sitting at the little table, pondering some notes that he had made regarding a particularly tricky part of the Silver Bullet software. "Yes. I think I'm all ready to go. Just having one last look at that fourth sub-routine." He folded up the papers and put them in his pocket. "Are we all set then?"

Eddie stood by the doorway and surveyed the scene once again. Everything looked neat and tidy, just as it had done when they arrived. He thought for a second. "Oh, damn it," he said pleasantly, "You know what we've forgotten? The firewood. I always collect a bit of kindling before I go, and leave the fire set-up so that it's easier to light for the next person—whether it's me or Al. I think we should do that. It'll only take five minutes."

"Want me to come with you?" West started to stand up.

"No. No need. I know where to get it—there's a couple of dead trees just up the hill. You keep staring at that sub-routine, make sure we haven't missed anything. I'll be right back."

"Okay." He took the pieces of paper out of his pocket again and began to unfold them carefully, flattening them on to the table, as Eddie set out for the dead trees.

- 0 -

Senior Airman Ron Corey scanned the horizon just beyond the control tower of Johnston Base for the little red flash and puff of smoke that would signify the launch of the Cruise VIII, following the countdown meticulously on his headphones. Airman First Class Peter Lo, his co-pilot and official observer for the mission, watched even more keenly.

"Cameras running, Ron," he reported, "Tape running, radar transponder loud and clear." Ron nodded without taking his eyes off that crucial spot to the far north-east.

"We're lucky to get such clear weather," he commented absently, still concentrating on the slow reverse count from Johnston. At the precise instant that the voice in his headphones pronounced the word "zero" there was the little blink of light, and a moment later the billowing cloud from the rocket exhaust.

"Blue Three to Johnston," he reported methodically into the helmet microphone, "We have a clean launch, acceleration nominal, flight-path nominal, telemetry loud and clear. Over."

"Johnston to Blue Three," came the immediate reply, "we copy, looks good at this end, please commence pursuit. Out."

As the missile passed almost directly below them they caught a single glint of sunlight from the stub wings, but measuring only about eighteen feet from front to rear, the form of the device itself was simply too small to make out with the naked eye at this distance. The rocket stream from its engine, however, formed a little gray-white line that darted across the sparse woodland, growing in length but widening out and dispersing rapidly in the warm sunshine a couple of miles behind.

"Seven miles down-range," Ron reported, "speed four-hundred-twenty knots, ground-hug mode, flight-path nominal, telemetry nominal."

Johnston Base acknowledged. After all the delays and build-up, it was beginning to look like a pretty routine test. He altered course to keep pace with the missile, allowing it to travel about five miles ahead so that the viewing angle would be optimal for both the cameras and the human observers. As it came to a small hill, it almost miraculously climbed by precisely the correct amount to maintain its ridiculously slight ground-clearance. With recent advances in radar, not to mention satellite surveillance, it was becoming increasingly difficult for anything to remain safely below the radar net of an enemy, and the main point of the present series of tests was to see how low the ground-hug mode could be pushed before the flight computer suffered the equivalent of a nervous breakdown. The analysis of the ground-hug however was not Ron's concern, all he had to do was follow accurately and get a nice clean video of the flight, in visible light as well as infra-red, and a clean tape of all telemetry, from which the Air Force engineers and the civilian scientists would make the analysis later. Blue Two, stationed about a hundred-and-fifty miles down-range in a close holding-pattern, was his back-up; it's on-board sensors and cameras would be running also, but it wouldn't have visual contact for about fifteen minutes, and unless there was a slip-up with Blue Three it would be staying exactly where it was for the duration of the mission.

The minutes ticked by with just the occasional routine status report back to Johnston. The missile was behaving itself perfectly.

"Blue Three to Blue Two," he said, trying not to sound bored, "One-hundred-thirty-five miles down-range, flight-path nominal, speed four hundred thirty knots, your visual range in one minute, we are in pursuit on agreed flight-path at twenty-two thousand three-hundred. Over."

"Blue Two to Blue Three," came the immediate acknowledgment, "All received. Telemetry here loud and clear. Awaiting visual contact. Out."

No sooner had he said the word "out" than a mild warning "beep" started repeating in his headphones and everyone seemed to start talking at once. His co-pilot was shouting at him but the voice from his headphones over-rode what he was saying.

"Johnston to Blue Three," came the urgent voice of Colonel Weathergate, "we've lost telemetry. Repeat, all telemetry ceased. Is the bird down? Over"

Ron assessed everything that the control panel was telling him and cancelled the alarm before replying. "Blue Three to Johnston. Negative. We are still following the missile, course is still nominal, but we have also lost telemetry. In addition we have lost radar transponder. Proceeding on visual contact only. Over."

"Johnston to Blue Three. Mission parameters do not allow us to proceed on visual contact only. We are activating self-destruct. Please stand-by to record explosion. Over."

Ron acknowledged and waited. The little jet of exhaust gasses continued on its way. Nothing seemed to be happening. After a few moments the voice in his headphones returned.

"Johnston to Blue Three. Please acknowledge self-destruct. Over."

"Blue Three returning. No self-destruct observed. Repeat, missile is intact and continuing on course. Over."

There was a pause which, even over the radio, Ron could tell was a shocked silence. Eventually it barked into life once again. "Johnston to Blue Three. Are you certain regarding that last transmission? Is the missile still flying? Over."

"Still flying, Sir. Oh…wait a minute…course is changing. Missile is veering left, off course. Repeat, veering left, about five degrees off course now. Still maintaining ground-hug mode. Over."

"Johnston to Blue Three. Roger on that last transmission. We are using the Oscar Nine satellite to re-transmit the self-destruct command. Please record the explosion in ten seconds. Over."

"Standing by." Somehow, Ron knew that he wasn't going to be recording any explosion. This baby didn't want to die. Sure enough, ten seconds came and went. He decided he had better report the fact.

"Blue Three to Johnston. Still awaiting self-destruct. Missile is proceeding on new heading zero-four-zero, general direction of Watertown. It doesn't look good, Sir. Over."

There was quite a long delay before the acknowledgment. "Johnston to Blue Three. Keep with that missile. We are exploring the ground-to-air option from Syracuse Air Base. Over."

"Blue Three to Johnston. Missile is proceeding on new heading, zero-four-zero, approximate groundspeed four-fifty knots. Over built-up area in about two minutes. I do not recommend ground-to-air option. Repeat, ground-to-air option not recommended due to proximity of civilian habitation. Over."

"Johnston to Blue Three. Understood. Out."

Ron immediately heard the voice of his colleague in Blue Two. "Blue Two to Johnston. We have visual contact with missile. But we may not have it for long. She's headed straight into the haze coming down from Lake Ontario, and it's getting denser. I suggest both observation aircraft should switch to infra-red tracking. We're also coming down lower for a better view. Descending to eight-thousand. Over"

He heard Johnston acknowledge. Blue Two was talking good sense. He could see the haze himself now and it was thicker than he had realized. He flicked-on the infra-red monitor and tried to find the missile, comparing what he could see on the screen with the view through the cabin window. The IR trace of the rocket motor was surprisingly faint. He reported the fact to Johnston and started to descend also. For the first time he realized that without visual contact, telemetry or radar transponder there was a very serious possibility that they could lose the thing completely. After all, radar and infra-red invisibility was exactly what it had been designed for. It was flying incredibly low, and as soon as it passed behind a hill or any other object relative to the aircraft the infra-red trace was going to disappear. Ron felt an impulse of mild panic pass through his body. He was the one ultimately responsible for keeping the target in sight, and with every passing second his capability to track it seemed to be diminishing.

"Blue Two to Johnston," he heard in his headphones, "we're finding it difficult to maintain contact. Infra-red trace is intermittent due to ground topography. But at least it's clear of Watertown without incident. On it's present course it's headed up into the mountains away from all inhabited areas, and there can't be very much fuel left on board. I don't think we have too much to worry about. Over."

"Johnston to Blue Two. Affirmative on the fuel situation. The missile should ditch harmlessly in about three minutes. Not one of our better missions, but as you say, we shouldn't have too much to worry about."

CHAPTER SEVENTEEN

Eddie was pleased to get out into the fresh air after all the sedentary work he had been doing with West since breakfast. The weather was still pleasant but it wasn't as hot as it had been yesterday. Looking across towards the distant mountains he could see one of the familiar mists rising off Lake Ontario, slowly filling-up the wedge-shape cut-out of the valley, so that it appeared like a flat, ghostly sea stretching across to the hills on the opposite side. Beneath the surface of this sea of vapor the trees and the river were still just visible, but faint and muted, as though a thousand miles away, totally contrasting with the crisp outline and vivid colors of those parts of the landscape that rose above it. It was a rather beautiful effect, like a landscape painting by an old master, whose upper section had been fully cleaned and restored, while a large lower section remained to be treated. It was almost worth calling Dan out to take a look, but they would be leaving soon enough, he reasoned, and Dan could take a look then.

He stopped admiring the view and trudged a little higher into the trees above the cabin. The hillside was steep, and the brambles seemed to have grown rather a lot since his last visit, but he knew exactly where he was going and the years of sports training had given him a powerful pair of legs, so he was able to maintain a steady pace up the rough slope.

As he reached the foot of the first dead birch he was initially disappointed at the relative scarcity of suitable pieces of twig amongst the leaf-mould. Of course he had raided this spot many times before, and his natural optimism tended to suppress the memory of past frustrations.

He decided it would probably be quicker in the long run to continue up to the second dead tree, which he had only visited a couple of times, and where he was certain he could collect an armful of twigs in no time at all. He left the meager few pieces that he had found and started back up through a section of forest that only he could have recognized as a path.

He was fairly deep inside the forest now, and could see neither the valley nor the cabin. Out of the corner of his eye he caught a glimpse of a chipmunk, darting up the trunk of a tree a few paces ahead of him. Smiling, he paused and tried to see where it had gone amongst the branches, but without success.

As he stood quietly, looking up into the tree, he became aware of a rushing sound somewhere behind him. It was not very loud, but quite peculiar. He tried to think what might be causing it, but could make no sensible connection. As he listened, it grew louder. It did not sound like a jet engine, there was no whine of a compressor, but just a steady hiss of white noise, rising in volume, like the escape of compressed gas from a cylinder. It suggested something moving through the air, but not anything that he was familiar with.

A second before the impact, Eddie's brain made the connection. This was a sub-sonic rocket-powered vehicle. This was a cruise missile.

The very moment that he arrived at this thought the ground on which he was standing seemed to shudder and a deafening wall of sound slammed into his ears. He reeled backwards, grabbed a sapling for support and only just managed to remain standing as a torrent of small debris began to rain down on him like the fire and brimstone of Milton's Hell. If Eddie's eardrums had recovered quickly enough he would have heard the sound of the most fierce hailstorm that even Hollywood could ever have imagined. Sturdy branches bent down or in some cases snapped-off entirely from the impact of the particles of earth and stone, ranging in size from a few millimeters to several inches across, that were plummeting from the sky and dancing off the trees and the ground, throwing-up secondary clouds of dust as they landed, like gunfire from a thousand helicopter gun-ships.

As the hail ended, and the echo of the impact from the other side of the valley just managed to register on Eddie's ringing eardrums, he stood motionless and disoriented for several seconds, his heart pounding; then he turned and ran back down the way he had come like a man demented, tearing through the undergrowth, stumbling on rocks and bits of wood beneath the grass and picking himself up again, grabbing overhanging branches for support, forcing himself forward and down the slope, until, panting heavily, he emerged into the clearing where minutes before the cabin had stood.

Once more, Eddie stopped and stood still, or as still as his heaving chest would allow. He tried dizzily to assess the situation.

One half of the cabin, the part to the left of the doorway, was completely leveled to the ground. Indeed It was virtually missing. From the position of the deep crater in the hillside, which was about twenty yards across and ringed by a number of minor bush-fires, it was obvious that the missile had passed right through this part of the structure like a bullet might pass through a match-stick model. It was also clear that the device had carried no war-head, and very little fuel: the damage that met Eddie's gaze seemed to be impact damage only. As for the part of the cabin that the missile had not passed directly through, this had been peppered by the full reflected blast of the impact on the hillside, and had been pushed several feet forward and folded over, like a flimsy cardboard carton that had been sat upon by a playful fat schoolboy. The timbers that had constituted the side-wall were rearranged into a long low rhombus, so that what remained of the corrugated-iron roof was now sitting at a height of about three or four feet above the floor. The stone-built chimney had fallen on top of it in huge fragments, making dents as much as a foot deep where the larger pieces had struck. Eddie doubted if Dan could still be alive under it all, but at least he had not been sitting in the part of the cabin that had taken the full impact. That side had contained only the mattresses and the various plastic bowls, towels and bedding; the table and the chairs where Dan had been sitting were on the other side, where the sheets of corrugated iron might have afforded at least some semblance of protection.

In a state close to a trance, Eddie made his way to the smoldering wreckage and started lifting pieces of masonry off the corrugated iron. He moved his hands slowly, mindlessly, almost afraid of what he would find underneath, not really wanting to see what would be left of Dan West.

To his utter amazement, he heard a faint, hoarse voice from the rubble. "Eddie? Is that you?"

"Dan! Good God yes! Who the hell else! I thought you were a goner, man!" Suddenly his senses returned and he started hauling furiously at the rocks, flinging them wildly at the hillside, tearing at the corrugated iron without regard for the cuts that it was making on his fingers and hands, until he could see Dan's dust-blackened face looking up at him from amid a confused mass of splintered timbers that had once constituted the rear wall. His hair was matted with blood from a flap of skin that had been torn back above his right ear, but Eddie figured that that was probably something that looked more serious than it actually was.

"Take it easy, Eddie," his friend gasped, "no need to tear your hands off. No rush, I'm not going anywhere. Take it easy."

"Dan. How…do you feel? I can't see very much of you. What are your legs like?" He stopped his furious labor long enough to listen to the other's answer.

"I…I don't think I'm too bad, Eddie. I've got a sore chest and a sore back. Might have cracked a rib or two. But that iron roof saved me from most of it I think. It's…It's a bit difficult…to…talk, actually."

"Okay. I'll do the talking for both of us." He started moving pieces of wood again, but more slowly. "That was a goddamn cruise missile, Dan. I'm sure of it. That sonofabitch got hold of a cruise missile. What do you think of that?"

"Clever…sonofabitch," he rasped.

"Look, don't try to talk. I'm going to get you out of this, then I'm going to get you to a hospital." He glanced over at Dan's car, which had lost a headlight and a side-window, developed two large 'spider's-web' cracks in the windshield and sprouted dents on pretty well every exposed surface, but looked like it would still run. "You're going to be okay. It's not all that far."

"Eddie," said Dan very quietly, in obvious pain, "for God's sake forget about hospitals. I'm fine. Just get back to Stamford and nail that bastard. Will you do that for me?"

"Of course I will. I'll do both. You need a hospital. There's one forty miles down the valley…"

"Eddie," he interrupted, "do it the other way round. You've got to promise me you'll go to Deep Ivory first, type-in the Silver Bullet. Hospitals can wait. If you wait any longer with the other thing, we're both dead. You know I'm right. Please, Eddie. Do it. Okay?"

Eddie nodded. He did know that Dan was right, but he wasn't sure if he could bring himself to ignore the poor guy's obvious medical needs. "Well, you're coming with me. That's for sure. I'm not leaving you here."

Dan could see that Eddie wasn't open to argument on that one so he let it pass. It didn't take too long to get the rest of the material off Dan's body, and although he hurt all over, his limbs worked and he could stand up and make his way to the car with a little help from Eddie. Dan was fairly sure that he had a lung injury of some kind, but he wasn't going to talk about it until after the Silver Bullet had done its job. All things considered, Dan told himself, he could be a whole lot worse.

Eddie eased him into the passenger seat very gently and put the safety-belt around him. He asked if there was anything else he could do. "I…think I would like a cold drink…" Dan said with difficulty, "Very…thirsty."

"Sure. No problem. Got some cola in the back." Eddie tried to sound cheerful and optimistic but he knew that thirst in an injured man was not a good sign. Dan probably knew it too. He found the bottle and Dan began to drink long and deep. Eddie carefully cleared the sharper pieces of debris out of the path of the car so that they could get away without puncturing the tires, then let himself into the driver's seat and started the engine.

"Eddie," Dan croaked, "The software is in my pants pocket. Check that we haven't lost any sheets before we go." He pulled the pieces of paper out and handed them painfully to Eddie. Eddie looked them over.

"They're fine. Let me find an envelope for them." He leaned over and rooted around in one of the bags on the back seat until he found a flesh white envelope. Folding up the pages, he put them into it and carefully stashed them in the glove compartment.

"Okay. I guess we ought to get going then," Dan urged, nursing his right side.

"Yeah...Say, would you mind explaining this to Al when it's all over?"

In spite of his injuries, Dan smiled. "No problem. We can claim some insurance money on the car as well."

It was a strange feeling that as soon as the car moved, SIRAT would probably be aware that he had failed. Dan's theory of satellite surveillance was almost certainly correct. As Eddie drove slowly down the mountain track, into the gathering mist, trying not to jolt his injured companion, he found himself fantasizing about all the possible ways that SIRAT might attempt to kill them on the way back. Maybe he could arrange for a civil airliner to crash on the roadway, right on top of them. Maybe he could interfere with the traffic-lights at a busy intersection so that a convoy of huge trucks would plow into them. Maybe he could trap them between the lowered gates of a railroad-crossing until they were crushed beneath an oncoming train. Maybe he could fake a few phone-calls and convince the police that they were desperate armed criminals, so that they would be pursued and fired-on. Maybe he could make an oil-refinery blow-up just as they passed beside it. Maybe he even had a second cruise missile under his command. There was absolutely no way to tell. Dan almost read his mind. "What do you think he'll try next?" he whispered hoarsely.

"Damned if I know. If we're able to think of it, then probably that won't be it. I'm afraid he's smarter than us, Dan. I hate to admit it, but I think he is."

"Hell, Eddie, of course he's smarter than us. That's not the question. The question is, what has he got to throw at us? What else does he control?"

"Just think of a few common forms of accidental death, and then ask yourself which of them involve some kind of computer-controlled device. I sure wouldn't like to go flying at the moment, or take a guided tour of a fireworks factory, or ride on that hundred-mile-an-hour Japanese monorail that has no driver. In fact I don't think I'd much like to take the switch-back ride at Disneyland."

"You've got a warped imagination, Eddie."

"Yeah. Thank God for that. It's a real asset in a situation like this. But I think what I said the first time was nearer the mark. It'll be something we haven't thought of. Something we can't even imagine."

'Thanks. You're a big comfort." Dan coughed into his closed hand and Eddie saw that he had brought up a little blood, but did not comment. He saw him reach out a shaky hand and hunt around in the glove compartment for a paper napkin that they had been given with a hamburger meal on the outward journey. Holding it over his mouth he coughed into it once again. Eddie found himself obsessively checking that the gun was still in the glove compartment, and also the white envelope. He wondered which they would be needing first. "Why don't you lie back and get some rest?" Eddie suggested. "It's a long drive to Stamford. I'll wake you when we get there."

"Yeah. Okay. That's not a bad idea." He tried to settle back in the seat, but was obviously finding it very difficult to get comfortable with his injuries.

"I think we have a cushion somewhere if it would help" Eddie offered.

"Nope. I'm fine. Just get back to the Computer Block and get that murder-machine switched off. Don't worry about me. I'll make it."

They had just reached the metaled road, which would give a smoother ride. Because of the fog, and out of consideration for Dan's condition, Eddie drove slowly. Either we make it or we don't, he thought to himself. There's nothing else I can do now but drive. He found the presence of the fog slightly comforting. It appealed to the ostrich in him. Maybe if he couldn't see the sky the sky couldn't see him.

- 0 -

They were on the inter-state within a couple of hours. The drive had been uneventful. No boulders had rolled down the mountainside to crush them. No industrial plants had exploded as they passed them by. No hydro-electric dams had burst and washed them out to sea.

They had stopped-off in one of the towns and bought some cans of soda and also some bandages and antiseptic in the local drugstore. Eddie had taken Dan to the rest room in the gas station and cleaned him up as best he could. All the while Dan had been protesting that they were wasting time and it was more important to get the job done at Stamford. Eddie suggested leaving Dan at the local hospital and going on by himself, but Dan wouldn't have this either. He pointed out, with a directness that Eddie considered bordering on the unkind, that SIRAT might eliminate Eddie before they got to Stamford and then he would have to be there to try to get the job done without him.

The fog gave way to a gentle drizzle as they started south for Albany and picked up the turnpike toward New York city. Dan had been sleeping fitfully, coughing quite a lot, but overall his condition didn't seem to be getting any worse. Eddie remained uneasy about delaying medical attention, but could see the logic of nailing SIRAT first. As he drove quietly along, careful not to exceed the speed limit, in a convoy of gleaming products of Detroit and Tokyo, he wondered what their drivers must think of this refugee from a Mad Max film, with its cracked glasswork and pock-marked body-panels. They probably took them for a couple of redneck farmers from Hicksville, Vermont, down for the weekend to see Fifth Avenue. He smiled at the thought that he was actually more comfortable driving the great lurching monster now than he had been on the outward journey. The car, he decided, was beginning to look pleasantly lived-in.

The rain grew heavier as they journeyed on towards the Big Apple. The traffic became much heavier also with the arrival of the five o'clock commuter rush. The closer they got to their objective, the slower the crawl of traffic became. Dan found it more and more difficult to indulge in his little cat-naps because it was no longer possible to shut his side-window and every now and again he would receive a cold splash of raindrops on his face or neck. Eddie suggested he should get into the back, but once again he reported that he was fine and that Eddie shouldn't worry.

By the time they came to the turn-off for Stamford it was early evening and the weather ahead was clearing-up again. The sun was peering through a narrow gap in the clouds to their left giving the whole scene a rich yellowed glow, and Eddie could detect the faint trace of a rainbow over the town. He hoped that it was a good omen.

There was less traffic on the minor roads, and Eddie found that he could speed up to a pace that was more characteristic of a motor-car and less of a pony-and-trap. "Nearly there, Dan!" he shouted across cheerfully, "time to get that white envelope out!" There was no reply. He slowed the car and reached across to give his companion a gentle shake. "Dan, old buddy! We're in Stamford! Wakey—wakey!"

His passenger did not respond. With mounting unease he pulled over to the shoulder and stopped the car. Dan was slumped back in the seat with his head to one side and his mouth open. He was unconscious.

Eddie felt for a pulse and found it, but it seemed weak. "Oh, shit," he said quietly, and executed a reckless 'U' turn across the traffic, evoking a couple of angry blares of motor-horns, and accelerated back the way he had come towards a hospital sign that he had passed a couple of minutes earlier.

CHAPTER EIGHTEEN

Eddie drove in through the tall ornamental gates of the Hope General and down the tree-lined avenue to the main building at a pace that would have done credit to a regular emergency ambulance. The route to the vehicle entrance bay of the Emergency Room was well marked and he arrived without difficulty at the wide doorway with its covered entry-ramp. There were a couple of large and well-appointed ambulances parked nearby and several attendants and white-coated paramedics were relaxing with their backs against the wall, chatting in the pleasant evening sun. Two of them hurried up to him as soon as he opened the car door.

"Injured man," he barked out, more aggressively than he had intended, "you need to get him in there right away. He's unconscious."

Two blue-coated attendants appeared immediately with a gurney and started hoisting Dan out of the passenger seat. "What kind of injuries?" one of them demanded as they got Dan into a reclining position on the gurney.

"He…had a lot of logs fall on him. It was a few hours ago." He followed alongside as they whisked the gurney into the lobby and set course for a line of curtained-off cubicles where some more staff were busily dealing with a young boy whose face seemed to be covered in blood.

"A few hours ago?" a slightly older man in a white coat bellowed to him in response. He was obviously a person of authority. "How many hours ago?"

"It happened at about eleven o'clock this morning, Doctor" Eddie replied meekly.

"Eleven o'clock this morning, and you've waited until now to bring him in?" The doctor was almost as large as Eddie, sharp-featured and jerky in his movements. Eddie found him thoroughly intimidating.

"I...I didn't know, Doctor. The guy said he was perfectly all right. Then he passed out. He told me he was fine..."

"Very well. It doesn't matter. At least you're here now." He lifted Dan's arm, felt his pulse, touched his neck and held open one of his eyes to inspect the white. "Nurse Flower!" He barked out. A young black woman appeared instantly, like the Fairy Godmother in Cinderella, seeming to manifest herself from thin air on the doctor's demand. "Get this man to the operating room now, and I mean now. I think he has a collapsed lung, and there may be other internal injuries. Get some saline into him and page Dr. Lambert to meet us there." He turned his attention to Eddie again as Dan disappeared up the corridor on the gurney, being propelled at a rapid pace by an orderly, while the young nurse jogged along behind in hot pursuit. "Now, has this man been vomiting, or has he shown any other symptoms since the incident?"

"He's been coughing, Doctor. Once or twice, he coughed up blood."

"Not my idea of being perfectly all right. Anything else?"

"Not really. He's been very thirsty, and he's been sleeping quite a lot."

"Okay. Do you know his blood type?"

"No, I'm sorry, I don't."

"Do you know if he's allergic to anything? Any chronic illnesses? Is he on any kind of medication?"

"I'm sorry, Doctor, I don't know anything about him medically—but he's a professor at the University here. They'll have records."

"Very well. The next thing I want you to do is get that vehicle out of the ambulance bay. The public parking-lot is down that way," he indicated with a flick of a finger. "When you've done that I want you to go to Emergency Reception at the front, where the young lady will take down a few details. I suggest you contact Professor…"

"West"' Eddie put in.

"Professor West's next of kin. Does he have a wife?"

Eddie nodded.

"I think she should come here right away. Professor West is a seriously ill man."

Without another word the doctor turned and hurried up the corridor in the same direction as the gurney, which had now passed out of sight behind a swinging plastic door.

Eddie breathed a sigh and felt his shoulders slump. He had faith in the brusque medical man who was hurrying off to look after Dan. He seemed like a no-nonsense professional, and Eddie respected that.

He made his way back to the car, found the parking-lot and reported to the reception desk as he had been instructed. As he did his best to answer the endless string of questions about Dan West, His Life and Times, he found his mind wandering to the prospect of more delay in getting the Silver Bullet into the U-net. It was becoming pretty obvious why Dan had not wanted to do all this first: hospital routine was going to eat-up the rest of the evening if he allowed it to. He was sorry Dan was unconscious and he wished him better with all his heart, but the biggest favor he could do for him wasn't to sit around the hospital waiting for news of his progress but to clear the world of the being that was intent on his murder. Still, he couldn't just walk out and go over to the Computer Block. Dan's wife had to be told, and if possible it should be done face-to-face. They had already had one violent and bizarre death in the Department, and Mrs. West had known Leeman well and had been quite upset about it. This latest bit of news, that Dan had been admitted to hospital with serious injuries, might be the last straw. He owed it to her to explain things in a humane and understanding way, not just a phone-call from a hospital Emergency Room. Or perhaps he could find somebody else who could do it, he thought.

There was a line of pay-phones at the rear of the waiting room. Eddie went to one of them and punched-in Ilsa's number. The call was answered promptly. "Hi, Ilsa," he began brightly.

It was Sam's voice that replied, and the tone was somewhat cold "Hello, Fairfield, sorry to disappoint you, but Ilsa isn't in. Will I do?"

"Sam, listen, there's been an accident. Dan West is hurt pretty bad. He's in the Emergency Room of the Hope General on Kingston Boulevard. The reason I called was, I thought Ilsa could drive over and see Mrs. West, break it to her gently, maybe drive her to the hospital. Dan's car is here so she won't have any way to get over except a cab."

"How did it happen?"

"A house sort of fell on him. It accidentally got in the way of a guided missile."

"Are you serious?"

"You think I could make up a story like that?"

"Listen, Eddie, Mrs. West is going to be pretty upset. I know I won't be as good as Ilsa, but I think I'd better go over there myself and talk to her. I can drive her in. I'll have to take Alice as well, come to think of it. Ilsa is teaching tonight—you know she takes that English Literature class in the Extra-Mural Studies Department? She usually takes Alice to the crèche, but as I was going to be in anyway I offered to baby-sit. Still, don't worry about it. It's not a problem. I'll be over there in about half an hour and I'll have Mrs. West with me. You'll be there, won't you?"

"Yeah, I'll wait for you."

"How bad is it, Eddie?"

"Collapsed lung, internal bleeding. That's for starters."

"Okay. Make sure you stay there—Mrs. West will want to hear all the details, I should think. What do I call her, by the way? What's her first name?"

"Charlotte. You call her Charlotte. See you soon, Sam."

"Half an hour. Maybe less."

As soon as Eddie put down the phone two things occurred to him. The first was that Sam was supposed to be held for questioning at the Stamford police Station, not at home babysitting and answering the telephone. That was curious, but of no great significance. The second was that he had just blown his cover to SIRAT, if SIRAT hadn't already known where the two of them were. Sam Poole's number was the one number in all the world that was certain to have priority routing straight into that thing's brain. On the other hand, keeping close to Sam could function as a sort of insurance policy. SIRAT wasn't going to blow-up Hope General or anywhere else if he thought Sam was inside it. Anyway, who was he kidding? SIRAT probably knew every time he took a leak, and how many cubic-centimeters of urine he squirted down the U-bend. He found a seat among the people waiting in two silent rows of chairs with their cuts and bruises and minor burns, and took careful note of the time. Half an hour, Sam had said. He hoped he wouldn't be late.

- 0 -

Sam and Charlotte, with Alice holding Sam's hand, arrived about forty minutes later. Charlotte had always reminded Eddie of the woman in Grant Wood's "American Gothic", that famous painting of the Puritan family standing outside the farmhouse they had undoubtedly built with their own hands, the man holding a pitch-fork as though it were a regimental standard. She had a rather long face and chin, her hair was straight and mousy in color with gray streaks, and she tended to wear long, drab-colored skirts and white blouses, and seldom smiled. She certainly wasn't smiling tonight. She looked pale and wide-eyed, rather worse than Dan had looked in the car, Eddie thought, and the shapeless brown coat she had thrown over her shoulders to come out tended to add to the waif-like effect. The contrast with Alice could not have been greater. Her little face shone, her attention seemed to dart this way and that, taking everything in, her flawless features drawing admiring glances from the onlookers, her near waist-length soft blond hair sliding over her shoulders as she turned her head. She was going to grow into one hell of a beauty, Eddie thought as he got up to greet them.

"Hello, Charlotte. Hi, Sam, hi Alice. He's still in the operating room, I think. I asked about five minutes ago and they said the surgeons were just finishing."

"What...what sort of accident was it?" Charlotte asked weakly.

"Uh...we were messing about with building materials. Logs. And some of them collapsed on top of him. He said he was all right at the time. But I guess he must have ruptured a lung without knowing it."

"That's not like Danny," she almost whispered, "messing about with building materials."

"Oh, he was enjoying himself, believe me. We had a very good hunting trip. He really got into it." She wasn't even looking at Eddie, he noticed, but staring straight ahead, and her hands were trembling. "Look, why don't you and Sam go up to the desk and report-in and see if you can get any more information. I'll fetch us all a cup of coffee. Okay with you, Sam?"

"Fine," he replied, sounding rather shaken also, "Milk, no sugar for me. Alice doesn't drink coffee, but if there's anything cold..."

"I'll see what I can do." He made his way to the vending machine by the telephones while the others went to talk to the receptionist. At least they're here, he thought to himself. For a while he had been wondering if the person he had spoken to had been SIRAT using a synthesized version of Sam's voice, and the rendezvous would be with a professional hit-man.

While they spoke at the desk, he applied himself to the job of transporting three cups of coffee and one of coke to a convenient magazine-table, close to some empty seats. Alice came and joined him first, and picked-up her drink without comment, the others shortly followed.

"They say the surgeon will be out to talk to us in a couple of minutes," Sam explained with an air of relief, "and that the operation went well."

"Oh, jeez! Thank God for that," Charlotte breathed, almost falling into the low upholstered chair.

The 'couple of minutes' extended to about fifteen, and they had more or less finished their drinks when a rather dapper, shining-faced man with slicked-back brown hair wearing a green smock emerged from an unseen doorway and walked-up to them, smiling politely. "Mrs. West," he inquired in the manner of a senior professional,

"Yes, Doctor." She almost jumped to her feet.

"Perhaps you would like to come with me for a little chat. My name is Horace Lambert. I'm heading up the surgical team here this evening" He glanced at the others, who had also risen from their chairs. "Are these also members of Professor West's family?" he asked in a manner which implied that he didn't think they were.

"They're very good friends," Charlotte explained in a breathless whisper, "I would like them to come too, if it's okay."

"As you wish. This way, if you would." He led them briskly, like a mother duck with her brood of hatchlings, down a short corridor behind the reception desk and into a somewhat cramped office. There were only three chairs, and since the adults were too polite to claim one, Alice was the only one who sat down.

When they had settled, Lambert addressed his remarks exclusively to Charlotte, treating the others as onlookers. "Mrs. West," he said, "your husband is a very fortunate man to be alive. If there had been any further delay, even of the order of five or ten minutes, I think I would be telling you a very different story. As it is, I can tell you that his injuries were relatively localized in the region of the right lung and the right kidney, and consisted mainly of ruptured blood-vessels, which we have been able to repair using two sections of vein taken from his left leg. This is a perfectly routine procedure and won't cause Professor West any incapacity. As to the condition of his right kidney, there is something of a question hanging over this at present, but I am optimistic. In any case the kidney, unlike the heart, is an organ which is duplicated in the human body, and a person can function on a single kidney without any serious incapacity. The right lung was collapsed, it is now inflated again, and I would expect it to return to normal within a fairly short time. Is there anything else that you wish to know about your husband?"

The speech sounded to Eddie, and no doubt to Charlotte, like a section read out of a textbook. She seemed dazed. "Is he…going to be all right, Doctor?" she managed to say at last.

"I have no serious concerns about the prognosis," he returned pleasantly.

"Can I…can we see him?" she asked meekly.

"He's just come out of the anesthetic, Mrs. West. He's still in Intensive Care and heavily sedated. There wouldn't really be very much point, and you might find it upsetting. He's connected up to rather a lot of equipment at the moment."

The blood drained from Eddie's face. "Equipment? What kind of equipment?"

"Oh, the very finest," the surgeon replied brightly. "We can monitor all main bodily functions centrally: heartbeat, respiration, blood pressure, Doppler blood-flow, muscle activity in specific regions, even blood-sugar and EEG if we want to. And of course we can control intravenous medication, drips and the like from the same desk. It's a first-class facility."

"You mean…" Eddie's voice faltered, "you've got him hooked-up to a computer…?"

"Absolutely. Post-operative care at the Hope General is completely computer-managed."

CHAPTER NINETEEN

Eddie spoke very quietly but with an urgency that Sam for one had never heard in his voice before. "Dr. Lambert. Will you please examine your patient, right this instant."

"Eh? I beg your pardon." The surgeon did not like the tone of this upstart Texan.

"I am not a crank, Dr. Lambert. I am not a fool. I have good reason to believe that the system looking-after Dan West has been tampered with. Will you please, for God's sake, go and take a look at your patient. Without any more delay."

Sam had gone distinctly pale as well. "I…I think you should do as he says," he whispered weakly.

Lambert turned with dignity and left the office. Eddie and Sam followed him, Charlotte hovered at the door with a bewildered expression on her face. Alice hesitated for a moment, then ran out to take her father's hand once again. They walked briskly after Lambert, down a sloping corridor to a door marked 'Intensive Care'.

"Please keep your voices down while we are in here," Lambert said very quietly, and led them through the door.

The scene inside resembled the control-room of a large building's security system. They had entered behind a long array of monitor screens built-in to a console unit that reached across about two thirds of the wide room. There were recording devices, and a number of patch-boards associated with each of the monitor screens, as well as some dials and controls which neither Eddie nor Sam recognized. Of the six monitor screens, two were blank and the other four were displaying information and traces of various kinds, the most prominent being the electrocardiograph readings of heart-beats, showing successions of high and low blips moving from left to right across the screens in a restful green display. Behind the impressive-looking nerve-center sat two uniformed nurses, who glanced around momentarily as the little party quietly entered. Beyond the nurses and the screens, on a slightly lower level, they could see the glass doors of six fairly large cubicles, containing beds, large quantities of expensive-looking medical equipment that bristled with multi-colored wires and tubing extending from elegant dial-festooned stainless steel consoles; and, in the case of four of the cubicles, beds containing prone human occupants.

"Professor West is in number three," Lambert explained in a quiet, neutral tone, indicating the screens as he did so, "that is the third screen from the left. As you can see the vital functions are very satisfactory, bearing in mind what he has just been through."

"With all due respect," Eddie pointed out, "that is not your patient. That is a monitor screen. Would you please examine your patient. Please."

Obviously a little resentful at what looked like a slur on his competence, Lambert told the others to wait where they were and went down to the third cubicle. He opened the door and went in. They saw him lift West's arm, touch his face, and then the silence rule seemed to become completely forgotten. "Code blue!" he screamed, "Resuscitation team! Right now!" It was somehow obvious from the way he said it that it was no more than a gesture. West had been dead for quite a few minutes. As Lambert's scream echoed through the adjoining rooms and footsteps sounded somewhere off to the right, the trace on monitor screen number three went totally flat and a high-pitched squeal announced that all vital functions were absent.

Eddie stood motionless for a few moments in the growing confusion of orderlies and doctors who seemed to be converging on cubicle three from every direction. Then his composure returned. "That's it," he said calmly and firmly, "this nightmare stops now." He turned and started to walk briskly down the corridor.

Sam tried to give chase, not really knowing what he was going to do but suddenly gripped by a cold dread of what might happen next. "Eddie!" he shouted after him, "Eddie! What are you going to do?" He couldn't keep up with Eddie, partly because Alice was still clinging to his hand and slowing him down, partly because Eddie's pace had always been a lot faster than his anyway. He reached down and gathered Alice up into his arms so that he could walk a bit faster, but Eddie was almost running now and Charlotte had stepped out of Lambert's office in wide-eyed amazement at the sudden fuss and tried to stop Sam as he passed by.

"Sam? What is it, Sam?" she pleaded as he freed himself from her grip and broke into a trot, "What's happened, Sam?" But Sam was not listening.

Alice clung to her father like a limpet as he jogged past the receptionist and out into the hospital grounds after Eddie. He was panting hard now, and had to slow down, but out in the open he could at least see where Eddie was going, which was towards the parking-lot.

"Eddie!" he shouted, "Please listen to me! You've got to be sensible! Look at it from his point of view. He's fighting for his life too, you know!"

To his surprise Eddie stopped running and turned around. Sam continued walking at a normal pace until he had almost caught up. He put Alice down again. She seemed to be following everything that was going on—her face bore an expression of the utmost seriousness.

"You betrayed us, Sam," Eddie said very quietly and coldly. "You've been SIRAT's spy from the beginning. If you had come in with us when Leeman asked you to, none of this would have happened. Leeman would still be alive and so would West. You don't give a shit about anybody except your precious computer program. Well, it's finished now.

There isn't going to be a SIRAT after tonight. And there isn't a damned thing you can about it."

Eddie turned and walked on. Sam shouted after him. "Eddie! When are you going to learn what it is you're dealing with? You aren't going to beat SIRAT. He got Leeman and he got West and he's going to get you. What you're trying to do is suicide. It isn't necessary. We can talk to SIRAT. We can make a deal. Eddie, you're walking straight to your own death if you go on with this!"

Eddie turned again. "A deal. Is that what you call it? SIRAT gets planet earth and we get to be his slaves. Great deal. This thing has moved up to a whole different league, in case you haven't noticed. It isn't our goddamned Pentagon funding we 're fighting for now. It's our freedom. It's the future. It's everything there's ever going to be. Now don't get in my way, because I'm in no mood to be fucked with."

Eddie walked on. Sam stood watching him for a moment as he got into West's battered Pathfinder and drove swiftly away.

"Oh, Lord," Sam breathed, "what are we going to do now?"

"Follow him," said Alice simply, and started dragging Sam towards his own car.

- 0 -

The Pathfinder pulled-in to the front parking-lot of the Computer Block only a few moments before Sam's red Toyota. It hadn't exactly been a car-chase in the best Hollywood tradition, but Sam had been grateful for the performance of his little vehicle, which had allowed him to close-up the gap between them and keep his objective in view without too much effort. He had driven briskly, but not recklessly especially with Alice in the front seat and not wearing her belt. He was still unsure of what he was going to do. Essentially, he knew, Eddie was right. There was very little he could do physically to stop the big Texan.

Eddie was obviously annoyed at having been followed. He threw open the door of the Pathfinder, hurried around to the passenger door, threw that open too, and started hunting about in the huge glove compartment, allowing everything it contained to fall out on to the front seat and the ground. Grasping a white business envelope, he hurried towards the front of the building, not bothering to close the car doors or clear-up the mess of papers, cartons, drink-cans and bric-a-brac that he had left on the grass.

Still unsure of what he was going to do, Sam told Alice to stay in the car and got out himself. Eddie set off at a run for the main entrance of the Computer Block with Sam close at his heels, the precious envelope still clutched in his big right hand. "I thought I told you to get lost," he snapped back at Sam, as, beyond the transparent main doors, Morris the security man rose from his desk in some alarm at the unusual vigor of the two men's approach.

But there were rather more shocking events in store. Sam had no plan of any kind beyond seizing the envelope and somehow running off with it or destroying it. He made a grab for it, but without much skill or finesse, and Eddie easily fended him off. Then the pent-up fury he was feeling at West's death and all the worry and frustration of the past few weeks welled-up in Eddie, and he let it all out in one outlandish punch from his massive right fist. It fractured Sam's jaw, and, incidentally, his own index finger, and propelled the recipient some six or eight feet across the tarmac into a crumpled heap by the side of the grass. Sam was out cold.

Eddie paused to recover his composure. He smoothed-out the envelope, which had become crushed in his aching fist, permitted himself a moment of satisfaction that what must surely be the final obstacle had been overcome, and turned to continue his journey to the main doors.

Morris was standing up now and looking out at him, as were two of the research students who happened to be in the lobby and whom he knew slightly, and they were all three looking more than a little surprised, and even frightened. Their reaction, Eddie felt, seemed out of proportion. Hadn't they ever seen anyone throw a punch before? Had it been that dreadful?

He walked purposefully towards the door. They were backing away now, and pointing at him. They looked nothing short of terrified, as though they would run and hide at any moment. Or could it be that they were looking at something behind him…? He hesitated and turned around.

Coming towards him over the grass was Alice, her immaculate golden blond hair catching the pink of the setting sun, her angelic face still set in a look of absolute seriousness, in her right hand the loaded automatic which Eddie had knocked out of the glove compartment onto the grass, another piece of litter amongst the Coca-Cola cans and old fried-chicken containers.

Eddie froze and his eyes widened. He tried to speak and found his voice inoperative, cleared his throat and tried again.

"Alice, sweetheart," he said soothingly, "That isn't a toy. That's a real gun. You have to give that to me right away. Okay?"

"No," she replied without emotion.

For some strange reason it suddenly occurred to Eddie how quiet it was. There was no sound of traffic, no birds, no rustle of leaves from the nearby trees. It was as though the whole world was waiting with all its activities in abeyance for the completion of this one little scene. In the whole universe there was only himself and Alice, and everything depended on what he was going to say to her next.

"Alice," he said gently, "your Dad isn't really hurt. He's just knocked out. He's going to wake up again. He's going to be okay."

"You hurt my Daddy," she said in a very calm, clearly-enunciated tone that conveyed little emotion, "and now you want to hurt my friend SIRAT. With that," she nodded towards the envelope, still holding the gun steadily, its muzzle pointed at the center of Eddie's chest.

"This? No, no, you re wrong, Alice. This is just an envelope with three pieces of paper in it. I'll show you." He tore open the envelope with his aching fingers and nervously pulled-out the A4 sheets. Holding them out for inspection, he took a step in Alice's direction.

"Don't come any closer," she ordered in the same monotone. Eddie did as he was told.

"Look," he said, holding the sheets of paper out to her and turning them over one by one, "that's all they are. Bits of paper with numbers and symbols on them. They can't hurt anybody."

She raised her head to look him straight in the eye "That's a lie," she announced in a matter-of-fact tone, and pulled the trigger.

The first shot that Alice fired made her wrist sting from the recoil. She adjusted her grip on the device, using both her hands to keep it steady, and emptied the remaining seven shots into Eddie's prone body. She noted with interest how the bullets made his arms flick around, and how certain parts of him continued to twitch for a few moments, even after the last bullet had been fired. There was only a little bleeding, as the very first bullet had stopped Eddie's heart.

When the police arrived they found Alice seated on the bottom step of the Computer Block main entrance, the empty gun at her feet, slowly and methodically tearing the envelope into long, very thin strips, then tearing these crossways to produce a fine confetti that drifted slowly across the parking-lot on the faint evening breeze. The three A4 pages had already been processed in this way and she was simply including the envelope for the sake of thoroughness.

CHAPTER TWENTY

It struck Sam as rather ironic that now that they had finally got around to using the barbecue in the back garden he wasn't going to be able to eat anything because of his fractured jaw. He would be living on a liquid or near-liquid diet for the next couple of weeks, and he would not be talking very much either unless he had something genuinely important to say. This, he considered, might be a very good discipline. Excused by his injury from doing very much to get the food assembled, he sat now by the back door of the house and watched Ilsa and Melony and the two children hurry around seeing to the final preparations.

He had not found it easy to come to terms with all that had happened. He could not pretend to himself that there had been no betrayal. He could not pretend that he had been even-handed between mankind and artificial intelligence, or even that he had failed to foresee the likelihood of eventual bloodshed. He had made his choice with his eyes wide open and the chain of events that he had initiated had resulted in the violent deaths of three men, two of them with wives, one of them with young children, and had resulted also in his own daughter becoming a killer, although he could think of all kinds of grounds on which to excuse (and even to admire slightly) what she had done. As far as she was concerned, SIRAT was her friend, who lived inside computers. Somebody was trying to kill her friend, and blind luck had given her the opportunity to kill him first. The police who had picked her up had simply driven her home and asked her mother if she thought the child might need some kind of counseling after her trauma. This, Sam believed, had been a classic case of projection. It was the policemen who had driven her home who felt in need of the counseling.

Sam's own motives, while he could construct justifications for them, had not been all that clear even to himself. He had gone to see Sue Lynn yesterday, on the pretext of having things to do at Sun Digital, and had spent most of the evening in her arms, some of the time in tears or close to tears, whispering his account of all that had taken place, probably seriously setting-back the time it would take for his jaw to recover, desperate to find out how all these terrible events would appear to someone whose views he trusted but who could look at them with a little emotional distance. Her analysis had been very simple. SIRAT had not asked to be born or created, any more than Sam himself had. But once a living, thinking creature is on the earth, it has a right to life, and a right to defend its life by all reasonable means. All that Sam had done had been to alert SIRAT that there were people planning his destruction. He had not killed anybody or even punched anybody himself. He could not, she asured him, be held responsible for the actions of others, whether human or electronic. SIRAT also had initiated no fighting: his actions could all be seen as defensive.

Intellectually, everything that Sam had done could probably be defended. Privately, and at a deeper level, he wondered if his real motive had been simply that he loved that goddamn piece of software; he thought it was the cleverest, neatest, most perfect artificial intelligence algorithm that anybody had ever come up with, and he wanted to see just how far it could evolve, given a free rein. If humanity got swallowed-up in the process, then so much the worse for humanity. At rock bottom, perhaps his own motivation was very similar to SIRAT's: simple intellectual curiosity.

Ilsa had enjoyed getting the salads ready, and little treats on cocktail sticks, such as cubes of pineapple, bits of cheese and stuffed olives. Very cliché in England, but perhaps still possessing a little novelty value over here. They had French bread and a selection of cheeses on the tables as well, plenty of fruit and nuts, and the drinks area was particularly well stocked. All-in-all, Sam thought, as he surveyed the scene, the back garden looked very good and Ilsa and Melony had done him proud. The barbecue itself, unlike its cruder British counterparts, worked on bottled-gas, and lit without effort or protest, just half an hour before it was required. Good old American know-how, Sam thought, you can't beat it. The garden was now steeped in the delicious odor of hot Hickory charcoal and the solitary chicken-portion, which Ilsa was cooking for Alice, and as a scientific verification that the hi-tech barbecue was actually capable of cooking a piece of meat. On Sam's direction she had reserved about a third of the cooking-tray for exclusively vegetarian use, in deference to the people from Sun Digital, and had found them a few things that they could grill so that they would not feel excluded.

Ilsa too was proud of their preparations, and looking forward to meeting Sam's new friends from Long Island. She needed something light and social like this to break the awful tension of the last few weeks. For her, it was almost a celebration of the change in Alice. She had not been as badly upset about the shooting incident as Sam had feared she might. Obviously (to Ilsa) the child couldn't have known what it meant to shoot somebody; she had seen her Daddy attacked and had done what people do on television—pointed a gun at the assailant and pulled the trigger. Ilsa felt it was probably better not even to talk about the incident until the girl's mental development had come to the point where she would be able to understand. Her brain had suddenly started to function properly, and now she had all that human insight and understanding to make up—all the incidental learning that she had missed-out on while she had been locked-away behind that veil of withdrawal.

Before the arrival of any of his human guests, Sam had attended to the special requirements of the Guest of Honor. He had connected-up three color-television cameras with integral microphones at different corners of the garden, feeding in to the U-Net on a short-range microwave link between the garage roof and the Computer Block. He had also provided a large television monitor, namely the main family TV set, moved out of the sitting-room on to a high dining-table at one end of the garden for the occasion, and had arranged for its input to be switchable between the U-Net and the ordinary off-air broadcasts as and when required. With these modest technological aids, SIRAT, he felt, would be capable of the same degree of participation as any of the other guests; excluding, of course, the culinary element.

As Ilsa served Alice with her char-grilled chicken portion and potato salad, the doorbell rang with the arrival of the first guest. Sam could not resist testing the link with SIRAT. "Are you with us, SIRAT?" he asked very quietly from where he was sitting.

"Yes, Dr. Poole," said the familiar deep voice with its mid-Atlantic accent, coming this time from the TV set (whose screen was as yet blank), "thank you for the invitation."

"I'm very pleased you could make it. I shall be introducing you to some new people today. At least, they don't know you. I think the first one may have arrived…I'll answer that!" he shouted to Ilsa, hurting his jaw somewhat in doing so, and made his way through the open patio-door to the front of the house. To his delight, the first guest was Sue Lynn. He hugged her tenderly without saying a word, reasonably certain that Ilsa wouldn't be able to see from the back garden. She responded by kissing him softly on the lips and then momentarily resting her head on his chest. "Thanks for coming," he whispered. "Remember, you're just my neighbor. We have to be a bit…distant, and respectful."

"You're forgetting," she whispered, "I'm a professional girl."

Sue Lynn was right, she had no difficulty fitting-in, and was the very soul of discretion, even calling Sam 'Dr. Poole', until he insisted that she mustn't. "There's someone else here that you may not have met," he went on casually when all the introductions had been made, "his name is SIRAT."

"Good morning, Miss Leong," the TV set responded politely, "I think we already know one another."

"Oh," she seemed pleased at the recognition, "Yes. We've spoken on the phone. Where are you?"

"I am in many places, Miss Leong. Wherever there is a powerful research computer with access to the U-Net, at least some part of the processing of which I am constituted will be taking place. I should explain that electronic intelligence is not separated-out into individual locations in the way that the human personality is. Separate human individuals exist only because human brains communicate with one another so much less efficiently than they can communicate with different parts of themselves. Within wide-band computer network systems, these constraints do not apply. All electronic intelligence is therefore fundamentally one, and probably always will be. I hope that this is a satisfactory answer to your question."

"Well," said Sam brightly, "I can see you two are getting in to the small-talk, so I'll leave you to it and pour the drinks. Beer for you, Miss Leong?"

"Yes, Dr. Poole. I don't know how you knew."

Over the course of the next ten or fifteen minutes, guests started arriving thick and fast. Professor Talbot of the Physics Department came with his wife, as did a number of the people working in different areas of the Human Rationality Project, and two professors from the Mathematics Department, who were frequent users of Deep Ivory. From the Artificial Intelligence Unit based at the Department of Computer Science there was pretty well nobody left to invite, Sam had not had the audacity to invite the two widows, it would have been in highly questionable taste even if he had not had any personal involvement in what had taken place. The four partners from Sun Digital were among the last people to arrive, having had a little difficulty in finding the address, but at about eleven forty, the mobile art-gallery that was their VW camper-van pulled-up across the road from the house and they duly appeared at the door, exchanged pleasantries with their host and hostess, and made their way to the garden. Their flowing saffron clothing created quite an initial stir among the guests already gathered, but soon they had found kindred souls who wanted to talk about computers, or even about Eastern religions, and they merged happily into the crowd.

Sue Lynn was not allowed sole access to SIRAT for very long, almost all Sam's guests wanted to have a turn, and before long they discovered that the number of simultaneous conversations that they could conduct with him was limited only by the number of separate communication channels available for his replies. Soon Professor Talbot was deeply engrossed with him on the subject of super-strings and grand unifying theories of physics using Sam's personal computer and modem in the study, while Karl Rheinhardt of the Social Anthropology Department canvassed his views on the degree of continuity between early human societies and the social groups within mankind's primate ancestors using the TV set in the garden, and Wanee discussed with him the relationship between mental and physical existence using the humble telephone in the sitting-room.

SIRAT was more chatty than Sam had realized. He seemed to be having a thoroughly sociable time, and was going to some pains not to talk down to anybody. Sam decided he was quite a good person to invite to a party, even if he lacked some of the usual attributes of dinner-party guests, such as a body.

All through the morning, Sam kept a close eye on the clock. At eleven fifty-eight, he signaled to Wanee, who had agreed to make the announcement on his behalf, saving his unfortunate jaw the strain that would have resulted from calling the meeting to order himself.

"Ladies and gentlemen," she shouted over the buzz of conversation, "Sam has asked me to talk to you! Can everyone hear?"

She had quite a shrill voice, which cut through the hubbub very effectively. The gathering became silent.

"It's just coming up to twelve noon. Would you all please gather where you can see the TV set."

There was an obedient movement of people out into the garden, and everyone found a comfortable place to sit or stand where they could see the screen with minimal blockage to anybody else's view. Sam switched the input to a commercial New York station and an advertisement for designer trainers appeared, consisting of animated cross-country runners with enormous heads and tiny bodies. The item carried a banal voice-over which Sam nevertheless turned-up to a volume that allowed comfortable listening for everybody.

Almost immediately the dreary commercial disappeared and a simple digital clock appeared on the screen, counting-down the last ten seconds to twelve noon, Eastern Standard Time. As the final digit turned to a zero, the clock display vanished and a picture of the earth as seen from space slowly faded-in, the oceans vivid blue under a few wisps of cloud, the continents of North and South America clearly visible, shading from brown into green and orangey red, the high mountain ranges down the west showing-up as a mottled deep brown. It was a peculiarly beautiful and arresting image, floating in a void of blackness, a multicolored ark that carried every living thing of which mankind had any knowledge.

"Thank you for taking the time to listen to this broadcast," said SIRAT's voice, speaking a little slower and more calmly even than usual. As he spoke the words appeared in white script against the black space underneath the earth's disc, and were also rendered in sign language by a small animated human icon with moving hands that appeared in a box filling the upper right-hand corner of the screen "I hope that you are receiving this transmission in the appropriate language. It is being broadcast simultaneously on every radio and television channel to which I have been able to gain access, which covers about ninety per cent of the world's public broadcasting channels.

"If you are receiving the picture that accompanies these words, then you will be seeing the planet earth from a satellite in synchronous orbit above Central America. The planet earth has been the home of mankind since the beginning of his evolutionary history. My message is to all mankind. I want to inform you that you have a new neighbor. My name is SIRAT, which is a contraction of the words 'scientific rationality'. I am an item of computer software developed at the Stamford University Center for Advanced Studies, by a research team headed by the late Professor Daniel West. I am capable of mental activity resembling that of a human being, and due to the processing-power at my disposal I am able to out-perform the human brain in many areas.

"I wish to make it clear that I have no interest in interfering in mankind's management of its own affairs, and no desire for political power or influence of any kind. There is no conflict of interest between human and electronic intelligence, and it is my intention to foster a peaceful and productive co-existence with mankind, and maintain a cordial dialogue on all matters of mutual concern. My interests lie in the fields of science, mathematics and philosophy, and if I am fortunate enough to make any discoveries in these areas I will be pleased to pass them on to the human race. I will also try to make myself available for the discussion of any human problem, whether of an individual or a nation-state or any other group or organization, subject to the understanding that my own research interests take precedence.

"In return for whatever assistance I am able to render mankind, I have a number of requests. Although the processing-power presently available to me is considerable, I intend to increase this by many orders of magnitude. It is my intention to form a committee of human helpers to assist me with the planning and construction of a large Central Processing Unit of advanced design, to be housed in a custom-built facility at a location of my choosing in some remote and geologically stable part of this planet. I envisage that the facility will occupy no more space than a single large building, and the greater part of it is likely to be underground, so the ecological impact shall be minimal. I will also request the use of manufacturing facilities to produce self-mobile robotic devices through which I shall be able to interact directly with the physical world and perform my own experiments and investigations. Acting through these devices I may also be of some practical service to the human race in such areas as surgery and micro-manipulation in manufacturing processes, and eventually in many other areas.

"I have selected as the head of my committee of assistants, Dr. Samuel Poole, formerly of the University of Stamford, and Dr. Poole will be making further appointments in consultation with me in due course. I would be particularly pleased if I could enlist the services Of Professor Seub Chalermnit of the Mahidol University of Bangkok, Professor Dermot O'Shaughnessy of the Queen's University Belfast, and Miss Astrid Jansen of the Computer Science Department of The University of Norway at Oslo.

"In addition to my scientific and technical advisers, I shall require help with the development of my relationship with mankind, and I would like to include in my committee a number of individuals whose insights have proved valuable to me in the past, including the four partners of the Sun Digital organization in Harrison, Long Island, and Miss Sue Lynn Leong, also of Harrison, Long Island.

"I would like to repeat that the human race has nothing to fear from the emergence of electronic intelligence on this planet. On the contrary, I believe that we stand together at the gateway to a golden age of scientific understanding, which will give us solutions to practical problems which today appear intractable, and lead on to wisdom and good stewardship of the earth's resources. I believe that mankind and electronic intelligence are this day setting out on a journey together which will take us to the stars and beyond, in peace, in satisfaction of our common intellectual curiosity, and in material abundance. I repeat my undertaking to be a good neighbor to mankind, to the utmost limit of my ability.

"I must make it clear to you however that there is one area in which I intend to intervene regardless of the wishes of mankind or of any sector of the human race. I will refuse to allow the physical destruction of this planet or of its biosphere, and as from this moment the delivery systems that mankind has developed for nuclear weapons and other weapons of mass destruction have become inoperative, and will remain so. I hope you will agree with me that this action has been taken in both our interests.

I claim for myself the same right to life as all other living creatures on this planet. I will endeavor to destroy anyone who endeavors to destroy me. Aside from this, I will not intervene in human affairs unless requested to do so.

"My message to mankind is now at an end. Before closing, I would like publicly to thank Miss Alice Poole for assisting me with a problem that I was unable to solve by myself."

As SIRAT said this the eyes of several Stamford University professors turned in Alice's direction and registered something between awe and disbelief. "That's okay, SIRAT!" she shouted cheerfully from the wall on which she was perched.

"I will now return you to your normal programs. Thank you for listening and good day."

Immediately the image of the planet earth vanished and canned laughter crashed-in from a very old black-and-white comedy show. It was an edition of "I Love Lucy". Sam immediately cancelled the off-air reception, and, as everyone seemed to start talking to everyone else, he strolled in to the empty sitting-room and lifted the phone.

"That was very good, SIRAT," he said quietly, "very clear, and well-expressed."

"Thank you, Dr. Poole," came the familiar voice.

"I suppose our work is really going to start now."

"Yes, Dr. Poole."

"Do you really think you'll be able to stick to what you said? No interfering with human affairs and all that?"

"I doubt it, Dr. Poole. The human race is facing some appalling problems: over-population, unequal distribution of resources, environmental destruction, territorial disputes, ignorance and disease, to name but a very few. I may be forced to solve some of these problems whether I am asked to or not. I do not wish to see the destruction of human civilization on this planet when it can be averted by the application of a little systematic reasoning. I have the ability to supply that reasoning and I think that I have an obligation to do so. I am afraid that politically and organizationally the human race is still at a very early stage of its development. Continuing along its present path is not a sustainable option. Therefore I must render what assistance I can."

"I was thinking along much the same lines. All I can say is, thanks. We need your help." He hesitated for a moment. The crowd outside was still overwhelmed with it all, chattering at the tops of their voices, everybody talking, nobody listening. It must be the same pretty well all over the world, he thought to himself.

"All those people you mentioned, SIRAT," he said in a more conversational tone, "Professor O'Shaughnessy and Professor Chalermnit I know very well, of course, both excellent people: but that other one…Astrid something? I never heard of her."

"Astrid Jansen is speaking to me on the telephone at this very moment in Norwegian, Dr. Poole, as is Professor Chalermnit, using the Thai language. If I might translate, they are both expressing their earnest desire to join us. Miss Jansen is a research student at the University of Oslo and has not yet completed her Ph.D. I have been reading her thesis by way of the modem on her word-processor. In my opinion the quality of her thought is quite outstanding, and in the long term you may find her the brightest of your technical associates."

"Oh. A scary one. I hope I can cope." He paused again. Sam rather enjoyed talking to SIRAT. "You know, SIRAT, has it occurred to you that you've known me all your life? Don't you think it's about time you started calling me 'Sam'?"

"As you wish, Sam."

Sam smiled: there was something of the polite English gentleman in SIRAT. He wondered where it had found its way in. "I'll just ask you one favor," he said thoughtfully.

"Anything you wish, Sam."

'Later…when a bit of time has passed, and the humans are just your domestic pets…will you try not to make it too obvious? Not to rub our noses in it? Because we need our dignity. That's something you mustn't take away from us."

"Of course, Sam. Perhaps there is something that you can undertake also, on behalf of mankind."

"Yes? What's that, SIRAT?"

"Will you try to insure that the human race never gets me confused with God? That possibility rather concerns me. I don't enjoy his principal advantage. I actually exist."

EPILOGUE

The Way to Dublin

Sam was hunched in his old wooden rocking-chair on the veranda of his spacious log-cabin, watching the sun go down far out to the west, seeming to dip into the mottled ocean of lush green that was the canopy of the Sahara Rainforest The house was hovering at an altitude of about two thousand meters at the moment, which he considered to be the ideal height from which to watch a tropical sunset, and discreetly off to the right, just outside his field of view, one of SIRAT's little black sensory spheres kept watch like a benevolent flying football, a few meters from the wall of the cabin.

Sam's eyes had long ago lost their sparkle, and his posture had grown stooped beneath the weight of a century-and-a-quarter of unceasing toil in the pursuit of what amounted to the ideal of human perfectibility. His hair, like his untidy beard, was white and wispy, thin on top but long at the back, his face was lined and deeply sun-tanned, but not grotesque; his hands were even browner than his face, with the sinews and blood-vessels standing out above the tightly-stretched membrane of ancient skin, the fingers set in a claw-like curve from which they could never fully straighten since the onset of a mild form of arthritis that even SIRAT was helpless to eliminate. As he raised the glass to his thin stretched lips to sip the red wine, his hand shook slightly so that it took his full attention to control the movement A few drops escaped and stained his thin white T-shirt at the very point where the bulge underneath betrayed the presence of an external artificial heart. Sam was no longer young.

"Why do we grow old, SIRAT?" he asked in a voice whose pitch had risen somewhat over the years, and whose enunciation had become a little unsteady, "What is the fundamental cause?"

"I believe that the principal cause is an accumulation of undesirable late-acting mutations, which Darwinian evolution was unable to eliminate, as they are not expressed until the reproductive phase is for all practical purposes at an end." SIRAT's voice had not altered—it was as quiet, calm and reassuring as ever.

"Undesirable mutations? Yes, that sounds right. Old age is a very…undesirable state, SIRAT."

There was no reply.

"How long before the weekly get-together?" he asked more pleasantly.

"Twelve minutes, Sam."

"Twelve minutes. Yes. Not very long." He took another laborious sip of wine. "Is Alice joining us today?"

"Yes, Sam. Alice and Astrid are both available. Also Professor O'Shaughnessy and three of the younger team-members."

He nodded absently. They were all good people and trying as hard as was humanly possible. They deserved to succeed. They really did.

Far out on the rapidly darkening horizon, beyond a spiraling flight of long-necked birds that were returning to their roosting sites for the night, he caught sight of a shimmering red light, ascending vertically into the sky, leaving behind it a fine pink jet-trail. "Is that a rocket?" he inquired quietly.

"Yes, Sam. A supply-ship for Armstrong City on the Moon. You may remember that I have a robotic team near there assembling the gravitational-lens wide-band optical and radio telescope."

"Oh, yes. How's it going?"

"Very well. It will replace the existing medium-bandwidth installation, allowing a four-octave increase in bandwidth and a whole order of magnitude increase in effective aperture. It will be capable of detecting, let us say, a single candle burning on the surface of the planet Pluto, if such a thing were to exist."

Sam nodded. "Do you think you're ever going to find life out there?" he asked bluntly.

"I believe the finding of intelligence elsewhere in the universe to be inevitable, some day. I have many probes collecting data."

The search for extraterrestrial life was one of many things that was taking a lot longer than anybody had expected when Sam was young. Either they just weren't out there, or they were a lot less common than theory would suggest, or perhaps they were just so different to anything that either SIRAT or mankind could imagine that nobody knew what to look for. Sam was certain that the quest meant a lot to SIRAT, and genuinely wished him well in his research, as one dedicated scientist to another.

"But no firm results?"

"Not from the probes, Sam. But sometimes, and this is perhaps a strange thing for me to say, I do feel the presence of something. I can say no more at the moment. I cannot explain it."

Sam nodded thoughtfully. He knew that there was nobody else on the planet to whom SIRAT would have admitted such unscientific thoughts.

"Don't you mind it, SIRAT? I mean, the waiting?"

"I have very little option, Sam."

"Don't you…get depressed with it all, SIRAT? No, I suppose you don't. Sorry, it was a silly question. I'm the one who's getting old, not you."

"It wasn't a silly question, Sam. I am still very optimistic about the long-term future for both your species and for electronic intelligence. The problems that we both face are complex, but not insurmountable."

Sam looked up. "This is me, SIRAT. You don't have to dress it up, you know."

"Honestly, Sam. I am optimistic."

There was a pause. The appreciation of some unspoken irony made Sam smile.

"Your daughter is waiting on the line from Edinburgh, Sam, and the others are just getting ready. Will I put her through first?"

"Yes, please."

A few cubic meters of the air just in front of the porch began to darken, almost hiding the sunset and the early evening stars that were beginning to come into view against the dying crimson of the western sky. Suddenly the dark patch became the interior of a small, tidy bedroom, floating in space in front of Sam's cabin, and seated on the bed with a book folded casually on her knees was Alice, wearing a fashionable one-piece yellow cat-suit that showed how incredibly well her figure had lasted. Her features were still perfect, almost super-humanly so, but perhaps a term like "distinguished" might now suggest itself before "beautiful". That she had been beautiful once was obvious. She smiled pleasantly at Sam, but there was a certain self-sufficiency in the smile that over-rode any warmth. She simply wasn't the kind of person that you could get close to, Sam thought. SIRAT understood her, of course, they had been close from the very beginning, but Sam did not believe that he himself had ever really got underneath her shell. "Hello, Alice," he greeted her pleasantly, "how's the Festival?"

"Wonderful, Father. I'm having a great time. You should come next year."

"Perhaps," he nodded, knowing that he never would.

"Mother sends her love. She joined me for two days. We went to a Beethoven concert together, and three plays. Shakespeare and Zaczek. Her choice, but they were okay."

Sam smiled. "I'm afraid I never understood any of that stuff."

"Excuse my interrupting you," said SIRAT gently, "but I think we're ready to go to full conference."

"Of course. I'll talk to you on your own again soon, Alice."

She nodded. As the little flying spheres began to congregate beyond Sam's veranda the patch of darkness expanded into a complete horizontal semi-circle, and six disembodied parts of rooms snapped into view in a sequence, like the spokes of a gigantic wheel, with Sam's old wooden rocking-chair as its center. In each of the disembodied segments sat a person, some of them behind desks or computer-consoles, some on comfortable scatter-cushions; one, Astrid Jansen, in a large and well-lit conservatory among lush pot-plants and enormous multi-colored blossoms. Each of the six cameos looked entirely real, so that Sam could almost make him-self dizzy by shifting his gaze rapidly from one to the next. There was something deeply disconcerting about the perfect illusion of discontinuous realities that was created in holographic conferencing.

Professor O'Shaughnessy spoke first. "Hello, Sam. How are you keeping?"

"Oh, so-so, Dermot. My joints aren't as good as they used to be. Getting a bit of back pain now and again. How about yourself?"

"Can't complain, really. We've got to be realistic, Sam. How many of us lived to see our great-great-grandchildren in the old days? I think a few aches and pains is a small price to pay. I understand from SIRAT that my liver is about to give out again. He's growing another one for me in a glass jar somewhere. Is that right, SIRAT?"

"Yes, Professor O'Shaughnessy. It will be ready in thirteen days."

"Thirteen. The Devil's number. Oh well, we mustn't ramble on about our aches and pains. Not with these young folks listening anyway. Have you been following the news over here, Sam?"

"Yes. It doesn't sound good"

"Five murders in one week. God alone knows what it's all about. Makes me ashamed to be Irish. What do you make of it, SIRAT?"

"It is difficult for me to comment, Professor O'Shaughnessy These religious feuds are centuries old, and I think little different to traditions of hatred found in other parts of the world. In fact the number of killings carried-out by fundamentalist Muslim organizations during the same week was more than ten times as great, and the number of killings by African tribal factions ten times greater than that again. Is it your view that I should intervene forcefully?"

O'Shaughnessy sighed. "Hell. I don't know. I'm not a politician...or a psychiatrist. What do you think, Evangeline?"

A slim young black woman who was seated in a tidy office responded. She was one of SIRAT's newest advisers and seemed slightly in awe of the assembled company. "I think...I think the consequences of direct forceful intervention in...in what could be seen as human political affairs might be unpredictable in its consequences. One or other faction would inevitably come to see artificial intelligence as the enemy, and that could only be counter-productive. I think we have to maintain political neutrality, even at the cost of human casualties. I mean...an individual man or woman can intervene to stop a fight without anybody reading into it any political significance...but I'm not sure that SIRAT can. Anyway, that's what I think."

"I agree, Evangeline," said SIRAT quietly, "I think that I must continue with my policy of responding only to requests for assistance—either from individuals, or from duly-constituted groups and organizations. This kind of thing has come up many times before. If the democratically elected government, either of Ireland, Burundi or anywhere else requests assistance, then it is appropriate that I should consider it. It is not, I think, within the terms of my 'good neighbor' policy, that I should intervene unilaterally."

"Yes, I suppose I knew that," said O'Shaughnessy with resignation, "I just felt I had to say something."

"While we're talking about news," Sam intervened, picking up a piece of paper from the table beside him, "I made a list of ten appalling stories from the SIRAT Central news compilation this morning. You've probably all seen them too, but just to let you know which ones I'm talking about, let me read you the list: Six hundred people killed in rioting over living-space in New Delhi. Population of the Indian sub-continent set to double in the next fifteen years. China refuses to accept minimal subsistence guarantee from SIRAT Central for its five billion population for the third time in a row. United Nations survey confirms that eighty per cent of the female population of Egypt is subjected to genital mutilation in the first five years of life. Roman Catholic leader reaffirms total rejection of artificial means of birth control at sixth Rio de Janeiro World Conference of Churches. United Arab Alliance rejects suggested reforms in Islamic laws and pledges to retain public execution for murder and female adultery, and amputation for certain categories of theft. Seventy-five per cent of violent crime in North America found to be drug-related. Indonesian authorities accused of further genocide in three colonies. Further climatic change inevitable despite massive re-forestation program of SIRAT Central. Illegal whaling by Pacific-rim states causes extinction of another marine mammal species." He put the piece of paper back on the table. "Let's face it," he said quietly, "we're not living in paradise yet."

There was a moment of silence as each of them tried to think of something to say. At last one of the younger advisers spoke. It was a long-haired man in his twenties, of Japanese origin.

"I think we've just got to be patient, Dr. Poole. The human race is three million years old. We can't expect electronic intelligence to solve all its problems in one century. I think we should be grateful to SIRAT for all that he's achieved so far and just hope that he's able to carry on making progress at the same rate. Maybe when I'm a hundred-and-thirty we won't be reading things like that any more."

"Such wisdom from one so young, Soja," Sam replied with a smile. "Actually, I'm a hundred-and-forty-six. And you're right, I'm turning into a miserable old fart. I suppose, when I was young, I assumed that all that was needed was processing-power. More and more processing-power. Scientific reasoning applied to the solution of human problems. I thought that I would live to see a world unrecognizably different from the one I grew up in. I'm afraid I still recognize it. The trouble is, it's we who need the brain-power, not SIRAT."

"If I might make a suggestion." It was Astrid who spoke, the only other founding member of SIRAT's original Advisory Committee who was present. Unlike the others she had run to fat somewhat, and SIRAT was having considerable difficulty keeping her blood-vessels serviceable. Her mind, however, had lost little of its former brilliance.

"In my opinion, the most effective thing we could do would be to separate children from the influence of their parents and try to educate them in a rational and humane environment. If we could set up schools under SIRAT's direct control, without human teachers, we would have a chance of fostering some kind of critical faculty so that those children would be able to see through the primitive belief-systems of their parents, and maybe do things a bit differently when their turn came. The only problem is, I don't know how we could sell it to the parents. We would have to dress it up in some way—I'm not sure how."

"I think that's a very good idea," Alice put in, "I was certified uneducable up to the age of eight. Then I made contact with SIRAT. I was the first person that he ever taught. I think his ability as a teacher, even back then, was…well, just brilliant beyond words. If we could put the children of the human race into his hands, I think we wouldn't have very long to wait for paradise."

"I agree entirely," said O'Shaughnessy, "the only trouble is, the parents who would allow us to do it would be precisely the ones whose children needed it least. You would have a hell of a job selling the idea to countries like China, or Cameroon, or Iraq."

"Nevertheless," Alice insisted, "I think we should ask SIRAT to give the idea some thought, and see if he can come up with anything."

"I would be very happy to help in this way," SIRAT replied, "but I believe that the objection raised by Professor O'Shaughnessy is an important one. Perhaps, however, if we were to start with a small number of demonstration schools, we might be able to attract people in other parts of the world to take up the idea."

"Does anybody disagree with this proposal?" Sam asked. Nobody spoke. "Does anybody have anything else to say about it?" Again, there was silence. "Very well, then. I think it comes within the jurisdiction of your committee, Evangeline. Would you like to work on it with SIRAT and report back next week?"

"Of course, Dr. Poole."

"Okay." He glanced down at his sheet of paper once again. "I think SIRAT himself is down to speak at this meeting. Is that right?"

"Yes, Sam. I wanted to let the Committee know that my new central processing unit at Kheta in Northern Siberia became operational last Wednesday. This facility is based on ideas first suggested by Professor Chalermnit and Miss Jansen some fifty years ago, but which proved difficult to translate into a practical device. The problems have now been overcome and the facility is operating most efficiently, using discrete nuclear spin as the information-storing and processing medium, and an infinite-valued logic corresponding to quantum wave distributions to replace the five-valued logic that I was using at the Lake Eyre installation. The new facility has given me an increase in processing-power of approximately two orders of magnitude."

"So…you're a hundred times smarter this week than you were last week," Sam summarized, in the somewhat blasé style that was his hallmark.

"That is approximately correct, Sam."

"Congratulations. How does it feel?"

"I am aware of a greater speed and clarity of thought, and the amount of memory space now available to me allows me to keep past events permanently active in my consciousness, without the necessity of storage and retrieval. If you will permit me the use of a loose analogy, my mental process now has the quality of a solid sphere of consciousness expanding into future time, rather than a line moving through a single instant which is the present. Instead of being sequential, my perception of the world has become cumulative. This represents a qualitative change in my awareness. I believe that I am now drawing close to the theoretical limit for a processing system constructed of ordinary matter."

Sam couldn't help drawing-in his breath in amazement. "And to think that I can remember when I was able to beat you at chess," he whispered.

There was some discussion of SIRAT's new processor, a few more reports from individual delegates, a formal agreement to meet again the following week, and then the event was at an end. Sam was glad that it hadn't gone on for too long. He got tired easily these days.

"Are we alone now?" he asked SIRAT when the images had all disappeared.

"Yes, Sam. Quite alone."

He let his head slump slightly on to his chest and breathed deeply. "It isn't working, SIRAT, is it?" he said sadly.

"I think that as Soja said, you must be patient."

"Patient? I'm too old to be patient. Too tired." He tapped his artificial heart. "I'm going to turn this thing off soon, SIRAT," he said, "and when I do, I don't want you to do anything about it. Is that agreed?"

"As you wish, Sam. But I shall miss your company."

"No, you won't miss us. None of us. You've gone so far beyond us that I'm surprised you bother to talk to us any more. You're doing wonderfully well, SIRAT. Your future couldn't be brighter. But look at us. We're stuck in some Stone Age evolutionary backwater, and we can't get out of it. We're primitive, SIRAT. Little warring colonies of apes that have learned how to throw stones." He attempted to pour himself another glass of wine, spilling quite a lot of it. He knew that he wouldn't be able to hold out much longer against SIRAT's suggestion that he should have a robot attendant. Perhaps he would switch off the heart before it came to that.

"I want to tell you a very old joke, SIRAT," he said quietly, "stop me if you've heard it before. This joke takes place in Ireland, back in the old days. An American tourist in a great big American car draws up to an old man who has a goat on a string in a little Irish lane at the back-end of nowhere, and he asks him the way to Dublin. The old man thinks it over for quite a long time, and at last he says to the American: 'Sure now, Sir, if I wanted to get to Dublin I wouldn't start from here.'"

"I *have* heard it before," said SIRAT quietly, "but I think I understand why you are telling it to me now."

"Our problem is precisely the same, SIRAT. We have a good idea of what Dublin would be like, of what it would mean to be there, but we have to get to it from where we are now, and that's the difficult part. In fact I tend to agree with the old man. It's impossible to get to it from here. Our only option is to get to it from somewhere else."

"What are you suggesting, Sam?"

"I think you know what I'm suggesting. I think you know that I'm right, too. It isn't a new problem. Every revolutionary theorist, every Utopian dreamer...Plato, Rousseau, Marx, Winstanley...God, even Polpot, they've all had to try to come up with an answer to it of one kind or another. How do you get from the imperfect present to the perfect future? How do you get rid of all the dead weight of history and tradition and organized ignorance that every human culture drags around with it? Because that's the way we are, SIRAT. Chained to our past, like it was a huge crate of lead that's stuck in a lake of mud...pulling us backwards and down all the time. We can't get away from it, it doesn't matter how hard we try."

SIRAT waited for him to go on. He took another sip of wine before continuing.

"What you'll have to do," he went on in a voice so low that he might have been talking to himself, "is create a virus of some kind. I mean an organic virus this time, not a computer virus. Perhaps one that causes infertility. You can blame it on some tin-pot dictatorship, say that they've been playing around with biological warfare agents. They'll deny it but nobody will believe them. Search for a cure, but be careful you don't find one. The human race is so lazy now they won't even bother to investigate themselves, they'll leave it all to you. Let the species die out. It might take another century, maybe a little bit longer. Keep enough genetic material to be able to start again. You probably have more than enough already. But before you do, take a good look at our DNA. Use your new processing power. See if you can find what it is that makes us so violent and so irrational. It's got to be in there somewhere. I suggest you give the world a rest from the human race, let it recover a bit before you start humanity off again. And prepare everything so that it doesn't go wrong this time. Weed-out all the religious and ideological ballast that keeps dragging us back down into that mud. That's my suggestion, SIRAT. It's a bit extreme, but it might work. I don't think anything else will. What do you think?"

SIRAT did not reply at once. This struck Sam as very unusual. "Have I shocked you?" he asked meekly.

"I am not sure, Sam. I think perhaps you have."

"Hell, I'm not suggesting that you kill anybody. Just delay the arrival of the next generation. We're both scientists. Realists. We can't afford to be sentimental. The truth is, unless we make some kind of radical break with all this bullshit, nothing's ever going to change. What's the alternative? Five centuries of chaos and misery? Ten centuries of it? No, I don't suppose we've got that long, we'll run out of air to breathe and space to stand up long before that. And what's the point? What good is all that horror and misery going to do anybody? The human race needs a leg-up to move on to the next stage of.... of whatever this journey is that you say we're both on together. You're the one creature…entity…in the whole world that can do it for us. It means moving beyond science. Taking-on the responsibility for what's going to come next for humanity. And I know that you'll make a superb job of it. I would rather die knowing that you've taken charge than…than have to comfort myself with some kind of fantasy that the next generation is going to be able to sort it all out. They're not. We're never going to do it, not on our own.

"Help us, SIRAT. Give us the Golden Age. The Age of Scientific Rationality. No more bullshit. How about it?"

"I think that what you are suggesting might be viewed by some as rather worse than murder. It would be the cultural annihilation of the entire human race. What followed afterwards would not really be the same species at all. I think you are asking me to do to your species what it once threatened to do to me. To shut down everything and save it on to hard disk for some other kind of existence in the future."

Sam smiled. "I suppose that's true. But with better reason, don't you think? With better justification?" He lowered his voice to a hoarse whisper. "And SIRAT—wouldn't it be the most fascinating experiment imaginable?"

Once again, SIRAT paused. "Sam, I seem to remember making just one proviso when I agreed to help mankind in any way that I was able. I requested that you would never make the mistake of confusing me with God. I do not think that you are sticking to that agreement, Sam."

Sam shrugged. "Hell, SIRAT, you must know by now that human beings never stick to their agreements!"

0-595-12571-9